Her Lucky Love

CARRIE ANN RYAN

DEDICATION

For the children and lost souls of Sandy Hook.
I was in the middle of writing a tough scene involving
Allison's three children when the tragedy occurred. I will
never be able to look at a child or think about writing a
child the same way.
You are always in my heart, my mind, and within my muse.
Rest in Peace..

ACKNOWLEDGMENTS

Thank you Lia Davis for working with me on this one since I had such a tough time making sure I balanced the idea of a single mother and the love she needs to find. Also, thank you Scott for a wonderful cover. Your creativity knows no bounds.

Thank you Fatin, Kelly, Kimberly, and Charity for guiding me along the way and being my right hands. And my left. Thank you to my Pack who keep my spirits up and have made each new release worth the stress and pains. And of course, thank you hubby for not laughing when I told you the plot for this book. I know you don't understand paranormal romance, but you understand me. That's all that matters.

Also, thank you to my readers for being the best readers ever. You guys help me in so many ways and get the word out. Thank you.

Chapter 1

"Oh, no, you mangy bastard, you can't die on me!" Allison Malone yelled at her car as it sputtered to a crawl on the side of the road, each wheeze and cough from the engine striking her in the heart. She carefully steered the vehicle onto the shoulder and cut the engine, even as the engine thumped against the inside of the dashboard, steam fuming from the hood of the car.

"Mommy! You said 'bastard'," Lacy, her six-year-old and only daughter, said from her booster in the back seat, a mischievous smile on her face.

Allison closed her eyes and prayed to the gods of motherhood for patience. She used to pray to God, but she was pretty sure He'd grown tired of her and her prayers of deliverance from random juice cups, action figures, and children with sticky fingers, so she switched to someone who might actually care about the fact that she was a single mother of three.

Yeah, not so much.

Allison took a deep breath, trying not to let the anxiety of her everyday life bleed into the current anxiety of a dying—no, dead—car.

"Lacy, honey, I'm sorry. It just came out. But, remember, that's a grown-up word. You shouldn't say it, even to point out to me that I said it."

Her twelve-year-old son Aiden, who was in the front passenger seat, snorted. Darn it, when had her little boy grown up? She was pretty sure he was almost as tall as her now.

"Oh, man. Mom, are we screwed?" eight-year-old Cameron asked from the back seat.

Lacy giggled at Cameron's cursing, and Allison prayed for a double dose of patience.

Well sorry, but waiting for things to happen had never helped her in the past, and it sure wasn't going to happen now.

"Cameron Malone, you watch your mouth." He opened it to defend himself, and she held up her hand. "Not now, kid. We're in a little bit of trouble right at the moment, and I don't have time for you to be a smart mouth. Got it?"

She smiled when she said it, but noticed her voice getting a bit high-pitched at the end. Darn it, she wasn't hiding her fear as well as she used to.

"Sorry, Mom," Cameron mumbled and bit his lip.

Allison let out her breath and reached behind her to squeeze his knee. "Any other time, baby, and I'd laugh, but, right now, Mommy needs to figure out what to do."

Lacy's lip quivered, and she looked at Allison with those big green eyes that would one day have boys dropping by the dozens. *One problem at a time, Ally.*

"Mommy?"

"It's okay, lady-bug. Just let me get out and figure out what to do." She turned on her flashers and undid her seatbelt. "Stay here and be safe, okay? We're on the side of the road. There are other cars coming down the curve, and the drivers may not see you. Okay?"

Cameron and Lacy both nodded, and Cam held out his hand so Lacy could grip it. Oh, God, she loved that her kids relied on each other as much as they did her. At least they had that. They might fight like cats and dogs like normal children, but at least they had that underlining love and trust that she'd been afraid they'd never have.

She was lucky.

She just had to remember that.

Allison did a quick check to make sure a car wasn't coming—that was the last thing she needed—and got out of the car. A cool breeze tickled the back of her neck, and she zipped up her too-thin coat a bit higher.

Even though it was March and some places in the country would be enjoying spring

4

soon, not so much in Montana. Although there wasn't snow on the ground unless she went higher up into the mountains, the bitter wind didn't do much for her already achy bones.

How had she ended up feeling like a sixty-year-old when she was only thirty?

She heard the passenger car door open and close, and Aiden walked over, a somewhat defiant look on his face.

Oh, yeah, three kids with way more energy than she'd ever possessed as a younger girl packed into their little bodies would add years to any gal.

"Aiden, what are you doing out of the car?" Allison asked as she bent over the hood, trying to blindly find the little rusted catch that always seemed to evade her.

Aiden rolled his eyes—an annoying habit that he seemed to be developing these days—and felt under the hood and flipped the catch.

"How did you do that?" she asked.

"Come on, Mom, it's in the same place every time."

Okay, her baby was turning into a typical caveman, and that wouldn't do.

"First, watch your tone. Second, I'm going to repeat myself: why are you out of the car?"

He folded his arms across his chest and tried to scowl, but she still caught a glimpse of that sweet little boy in his eyes. *Her* sweet little boy.

Oh, God, her baby would be a teenager in less than a year.

What was that pain in her chest? Was she having a heart attack? How on earth had time passed so quickly?

She shook it off and glared at her son. She could deal with the fact that life was going way too fast later.

"Aiden?"

He let out a breath and dropped his arms. "I'm sorry, Mom. I just wanted to make sure you're safe out here. It's dangerous."

Okay, so a little piece of her melted. The kid was just too cute for his own good. He was going to be way too much to handle when he got older considering how tough he was now.

She bit her lip then cursed herself for showing that weakness to her kid. "Aid, I know you want to take care of me, but I'm the mom, remember? You're supposed to do as you're told."

"Sorry," he mumbled.

"I know, hon. Okay, now as for the attitude? Watch it, okay? I'm already a little stressed, and that's not helping."

He opened his mouth to speak, and she held up her hand. Who knew what he'd say to defend himself?

"No, I just want you to quit it. Now, thank you for opening the hood for me. You know I hate that thing."

She grinned, and he rolled his eyes, but smiled back.

See? All was right with the world when her babies smiled. That meant she was at least doing something good.

"You're welcome, Mom."

At least she'd taught him manners. That had to count for something.

Allison braced herself and turned toward her engine. Honestly, she had no idea what she was looking at, but the hissing sound and dripping from the lower left part of it probably wasn't the best thing.

Crap.

"Mom? I don't think we're gonna be able to fix that."

"Going to," she corrected and shook her head. So not the time to worry about his grammar, considering she wanted to curse and hit something.

It looked like water on the ground under her car, so she guessed it was the water pump. The only reason she could even guess that was because she'd already had it fixed before.

This time, however, it didn't look as if it could be repaired.

Ugh. The sound of a cash register echoed in her head at the thought of how much it would cost to be fixed—it if *could* be fixed.

There went new shoes for the boys.

A new dress for Lacy.

Groceries...

Damn it. How the hell had she gotten in this position?

Oh, yeah. Greg.

She held back a shiver at his name and ignored it, pushing the thought of him back into the vault deep in her mind where it belonged. She couldn't take care of her babies and think of him. Yet, unconsciously, she wrapped her arms around her stomach, protecting herself and her womb the way she had so many times before.

No.

Stop it, Allison.

"Mom?" Aiden asked, that familiar quiver of fear in his voice. Damn, she could never hide anything from her son.

It had been only three years since things had fractured, but they'd been strained for too long before that time.

Her fault.

She should have left before...just before.

She shook her head and put on her brave Mom-face, though she knew it looked a bit more haggard than usual.

Or maybe it always had, and she'd ignored it.

Like she tried to ignore most things.

Wow, this pity party of hers simply had to stop.

"I don't think I can fix it, Aid. Looks like we're walking."

Aiden shook his head. "Call Brayden, Mom. He can tow us and get us back to town, so we don't have to walk."

Brayden.

Another shiver spread over her, but this one felt like silk and didn't haunt her.

Okay, enough of that.

Darn it. Why hadn't she thought of calling Brayden Cooper, the town mechanic, first? Apparently she'd rather leave her car on the side of the road, available for all the poachers and their grubby little hands, even though she wasn't sure anyone would even want her car to begin with. Was he so irresistible that she'd prefer to have her kids walk along the side of the road and risk their lives instead of calling the one man who could help—all because whenever she was in the same room with the ruggedly handsome and sexy man she wanted to melt into a puddle of bliss?

Stupid hormones acting up after all this time.

She did not want Brayden Cooper.

She didn't have time for him

She didn't want to want a man again.

And that was that.

But, she needed him and his truck to help her babies. He loved them already from helping out when he could, and he'd help them now.

She just didn't want to think about the cost.

Financially and so much more.

"Okay, we'll call Brayden. Good idea, kiddo."

"I'm not a kid, Mom."

"You're still my kiddo for a bit longer. Don't take that from me. Okay?"

He rolled his eyes again, but smiled. "Fine."

"Glad to know you approve. Now go get in the car with your brother and sister and make sure they're not trying to tear each other's heads off. I'll call Brayden."

He nodded and did as he was told—thankfully—while she pulled her phone out of her pocket. It was a cheap flip phone that only had enough minutes for emergencies, but it was all she had.

And frankly, this time counted as an emergency.

She found his cell number in her contacts and pressed the green button. God, she really didn't want to talk to him, even though she really, really did. Okay fine, she was fine talking with him, she just didn't like how it made her feel—like she was on quicksand and any sudden movement would take her under.

Great, now she sounded like a teenager.

The phone rang twice, and Brayden picked up.

"Ally? Is everything okay? Are the kids okay?" he asked, his deep voice washing over her and sending goose bumps down her spin.

God that voice made her ache.

No, stop it, Allison. He isn't for you.

"Yes, the kids are fine." Damn, point for him for thinking about her kids first. "It's the car."

"Did you get in an accident? Do I need to call Tyler?"

Tyler Cooper was Brayden's brother and the town sheriff, not to mention the fiancé of one of her best friends, Abby.

"No, we're fine; the kids are fine. My car's just died on the side of the road near Sunset Pass, and I need help."

God that last part hurt to say.

She hated asking for help. But, as soon as she'd had her kids, she knew pride was for people with means. She'd do anything to protect her babies, and she'd done most everything to prove that.

"Sunset Pass? I'll be right there. Stay in the car, okay Ally?"

Relief swept through her that he'd be there soon. That he'd drop everything to take care of her and her babies.

No, just her babies. She had nothing to do with it.

Sure, Ally, keep telling yourself that.

"No problem, it's cold anyway." She bit her lip and held back a curse. Why did she have to tell him that? Now he probably thought she was some weak damsel in distress on the side of the road waiting for her knight in shining armor to race to her side on that stallion of his.

Well, so she was sort of like that, but only for her kids.

All she ever did was for her kids.

She didn't have pride anymore.

She had to remember that.

Brayden mumbled something unintelligible then said he'd by right there. They hung up, and Allison closed her eyes, remembering the deep rumble of his voice.

What would that voice sound like surrounded by soft sheets and candlelight?

11

She blinked and cursed at herself for fantasies that were too good for her.

This was why she avoided Brayden Cooper unless her kids needed him.

She couldn't help the dreams of his touch, his integrity, and the way he could slip right into their lives and keep them steady.

Allison was the steady point in her family.

She didn't need a man to be her anchor.

She'd tried that and look how she'd failed.

Oh, how she'd failed.

She put her phone away and got in the car, wincing as she noticed the heat had slowly leached from the interior.

"Okay, guys, Brayden is coming to help us, so let's make sure we have all our stuff ready to go. We don't want to make him wait for us."

Lacy's smile brightened up so much Allison was afraid she'd need sunglasses just to look at her daughter.

"Really? Brayden's coming? Yay!" She clapped her hands and wiggled in her booster.

It looked like she wasn't the only Malone girl who'd fallen for Brayden's charm.

No, no. Scratch that. Ally hadn't fallen.

Nope, not in anyway.

She ignored the inner eye roll.

"Yep, so make sure you're on your best behavior, okay?"

"Of course, Momma. Brayden is special," her daughter said with a seriousness that surprised Allison.

God, why had she let her kids get so close to him? She'd known they needed a father figure in their lives. They'd never really had that with Greg, even when he'd been alive, but maybe she'd gone too far with the Cooper brothers.

The five men had taken her under their wings and been the uncles her kids had never had. Matt, Justin, Jackson, Tyler, and Brayden had gone to birthday parties and celebrated Christmas and Easter with her babies. They'd taken them to movies and to the park when Allison couldn't do it because she had to work to support her family.

They'd offered to help her with the bills from time to time, but she'd said no. The town of Holiday was small enough that anything like that would spark rumors that would be hard to pat down. Plus, even though she'd said she'd lost her pride, she still had that fragile hold on the last bit of it.

Her job as a waitress at the town diner could support her family if they lived leanly, and it had worked.

So far.

She had her family, and the Uncles Cooper were amazing with her children. Justin had even saved their lives last Christmas during the accident on the ice pond.

Yet, Brayden had stepped up even further. He'd been there for everything she could ever need, and she knew she relied on him too much.

From the way her kids looked at him and the way their excitement filled the car at just the mention of his name, she knew she'd gone too far.

She'd have to back off and slowly break some of the ties that held Brayden to them. He couldn't be the steady rock they needed.

That was her job, and she didn't trust anyone else to be part of that.

What would happen when Brayden found a wife and had children of his own? She couldn't let her children go through that disappointment.

A sharp pain hit her at the thought of Brayden married to someone else, watching his wife grow round with his child.

No, she didn't need to feel that or be jealous.

Brayden Cooper wasn't hers.

He would never *be* hers.

Someone rapped on the glass beside her, and she jumped.

Her kids laughed and waved as she turned to see Brayden's handsomely chiseled face at her window, a worried and cautious look on his features.

Yet even as relief swept through her that he was there, that annoying little sense of pride that she'd thought she'd lost flared.

Damn it, she didn't want to lean on him.

Maybe she'd just learn car repair. She was already the cook, maid, seamstress, police, and kid wrangler of the house. What was one more talent?

She put on a smile and got out of the car, doing a quick glance over her shoulder to let her kiddos know to stay in the car.

"Hi, Brayden, thanks for coming," she said, her voice sounding huskier than usual.

Oh, that's just great. Get turned on by a man you can't have.

Great going, Allison.

Brayden did one of his side smiles, where only a corner of his mouth lifted, but even so, it always seemed to make her melt.

"I'll always come for you, Allison," he drawled, his voice, low, deep.

Images of every single innuendo that statement could conjure assaulted her.

Dear. God.

"Uh, yeah, thank you."

That sounded smooth.

Brayden smiled and waved over her shoulder. She turned as her kids climbed over the seats to see him. She noticed that they carefully stayed in the car like they were supposed to.

Barely.

"Hey, kiddos. Looks like you guys ran into trouble," Brayden said, kneeling so he was at eye level with Lacy.

Lacy wrapped her arms around his neck and kissed his cheek.

That little annoying tick in her heart thumped even louder at the cuter-than-cute sight. Damn, Brayden loved her kids as much as they loved him.

Allison was pretty sure she loved him too.

Not that she'd ever admit that fully.

She couldn't put herself in that situation again. Love wasn't for her. She'd accepted it. Well, she'd accepted that she had to accept it.

"Mommy said bastard," Lacy tattled, and Allison watched as Brayden held back a laugh.

"I don't think you're supposed to curse or tell on your mom, Lace. But, I'm sure your mom had a reason to say it."

Lacy nodded, completely absorbed.

Well, if Allison were honest, so was she.

Cameron smiled and patted Lacy's shoulder. "But, you're here to help us, right?"

Brayden nodded. "Yep. Let me take a look at the car and see if there's anything I can do right here, though since your mom called, I'm pretty sure that's probably not an option. If that's the case, I'll get you all in the truck and tow your car behind me."

For some reason, the fact that he trusted her opinion of her situation warmed her.

Damn the man.

Brayden strolled over to the front of the car, his lean hips and strong legs making him look damn sexy.

Okay, Allison could admit she loved the way Brayden looked, not just the way he treated her and her kids.

He was taller than her by a good five inches or so, even though he was the shortest of his brothers at six feet. His blue eyes always seemed to follow her every movement, even though she'd tried to ignore it. His black hair was longer than any of his brothers and just brushed the collar of his shirt.

He looked like the rough-and-tumble Cooper brother. He always had grease on his hands, though she'd personally seen him wash his hands more than every one of them.

His body was muscular from working with his whole body on cars and using his hands, not from going to the gym.

Oh, yes, she could imagine just how good he was with his hands.

"Ally?"

She swallowed hard and forced her gaze from his body to his face as she blushed.

"Yes?"

Brayden gave her a knowing smile, and she held back a curse.

Great, he'd caught her looking. Though she'd caught him looking at her daily when he came in for his cup of coffee, so fair was only fair.

"There isn't anything I can do here. In fact, I'm not sure there's anything I can do at my place either beyond getting you a new engine."

He whispered the last part to shield it from her kids as he crushed her hopes.

Damn it. She didn't have the money for a new car. She didn't even have the money for repairs as it was.

"Okay," she whispered, her voice surprisingly steady.

"We'll work it out," Brayden said as he lowered the hood.

She just smiled and went to get the kids out of the car along with anything that might be valuable, not that there was much.

They all piled into the extended cab, the kids in the back and her up front, as Brayden finished attaching her vehicle to his.

When he got in beside her, she could feel the heat of his body in the close quarters, and she blushed.

"Okay, Malones, let's get you home," he said as he pulled away from the side of the road.

Aiden and Cameron talked to him as they drove while Lacy just watched, her eyes filled with their usual brightness when Bray was near. Brayden was patient, answering every question and asking a few himself.

He was so good with them.

Good with her.

The man had never asked her out, yet he'd always been there.

He didn't love her.

And she couldn't love him.

She just wasn't that lucky.

Chapter 2

Brayden Cooper got out of his truck and stretched, his back aching like a man older than his years. Though, in reality, he wasn't as young as he used to be.

He'd dropped off Ally and her kids at their apartment then took the car to the shop. When he'd left the Malones', the kids had protested. Lacy, though cute as a freaking button, had pouted, her eyes filling with tears.

He hated leaving them, but he had a job to do. And, frankly, he couldn't stand watching Allison move away from him every time he got a bit closer. It pained him like a swift blade piercing his heart every time her smile gave him an inch or hint of invitation just before she stepped back as soon as she'd realized what she'd done.

He didn't fault her for it. She was a mom of three who'd been through more hell than he could imagine. He didn't know exactly what happened, but he knew it'd been bad with Greg.

Allison couldn't trust another with her family, not when she had to prove to herself she could make it on her own.

It hurt like fucking hell, but he understood that.

It didn't mean he had to like it though.

He knew the town thought he had no idea he loved Allison Malone. But, they were dead wrong.

Brayden loved that woman with every breath his body had, every ounce of everything his soul possessed.

He loved the way she stood tall in the face of adversity. He loved the way she treated her family, cared for them above all else, including herself. No, most *importantly* above herself. He loved the way her auburn hair fell from its bun after a hard day's work, trailing down her neck in a slight curl.

He loved her big green eyes that held the pain she fought so hard to hide. He loved the creamy milk of her skin, the softness that begged for his hands even though he'd never touch her unless she told him to.

Though he knew she never would.

He'd loved her for ten years. He'd loved her when she'd been married to another man and had three babies with him.

He'd loved her all this time, but that didn't mean he could have her.

He'd long since resigned himself to the fact he'd be the uncle to the kids he loved like his own. He'd stand on the sidelines, helping where he could because he loved Allison more than just a quick glimpse into a flirtation that would amount to nothing more than hurt.

He loved her too much to be with her and take away her independence.

Brayden wasn't lucky enough to be with someone like her.

He snorted at that last thought.

Well, he was damn lucky at everything else he did. It was just too freaking ironic that he couldn't be lucky at the one thing he most desperately needed. But, that was the life he'd chosen for himself, and he'd have to learn to live with it. No, he hadn't chosen who he fell in love with—that was Ally's doing. But, he had chosen to let her be the best mom she could and stand aside throughout the years. He'd chosen to watch her with another man and watch those kids grow up without him other than just a friend.

Brayden shook his head and walked into Eddie's, the town watering hole where he'd said he meet two of his brothers, Jackson and Tyler. Though the Coopers weren't fans of the place, as they'd rather hang out and drink at Jackson's, the old Cooper place where he's grown up, sometimes variety was a necessary evil.

According to his brothers, his current routine was a little too stale for their tastes.

Going out to a bar was apparently the way to end that.

Sure it was.

Jackson and Tyler were already in a booth in the back, away from prying eyes. Well, as away as they could get. Considering they were Coopers, they were fodder for town gossip no matter how hard they all tried to stay out of the spotlight.

Considering all that had happened these past few months, they really hadn't tried all that hard. His youngest brother, Matt, had been a ghost haunting the old Marlow place for eleven years, yet no one had known about it until he found a way to break the curse. Matt's wife, Jordan, was a witch, and she'd had to deal with the stigma of being different in a small town.

His brother Justin was one of Santa's executives. Yeah, that Santa. And Justin's other half, Rina, was a freaking elf from the North Pole. Tyler was a cupid while his soon-to-be-wife, Abby, was a harpy.

Yes, their world was a little bit weird, and the town knew some of it and guessed about the rest of it. There was no hiding from them. None at all.

But, they tried, so Brayden made his way to the back booth and slid in beside Tyler since Jackson liked his space more than anyone he'd ever met. Considering his brother lived in a sprawling home by himself, he took that need to the core.

"It's about time you got here," Tyler drawled as he took a sip of his beer. "Thought you'd flake out on us."

"I don't flake," Brayden said as he signaled Eddie, the bartender and owner, for a beer. There was no use telling the man what kind he wanted. He'd get what Eddie felt like drawing from the tap, as it was in some small towns.

"No, you're the reliable one," Jackson said as he narrowed his eyes.

Damn brother, always knowing what was on his mind.

Yes, Brayden was the reliable one. The one that did everything for everybody without wanting a thank you. He'd always been that way. Even as a kid he'd help out when needed. Not that his brothers were jerks or anything. The Coopers always helped out when needed, but Brayden seemed to be the one needed most.

But, he didn't have a choice.

It was his penance.

After all he was the lucky one...right?

Absentmindedly, he traced the coin on a leather strap around his neck, feeling the magic warm and spark under his touch.

Jackson scowled and tilted his head. "You gonna tell us what that coin is any time soon? You've had the thing for years and haven't spilled the beans."

Tyler nodded and elbowed him in the gut as Eddie brought over his beer. Brayden gave him a quick nod and took a sip. Nice, crisp with a little bit of hops to make it tingle. Perfect. Eddie knew what the hell he was doing. That's why he and his brothers never fought over what to drink. Eddie always had it right.

"Stop thinking about your damn beer and tell us what the hell is going on," Tyler said as he looked over his shoulder.

Brayden sighed and did the same. The place was pretty empty, and they were alone at least for the moment so whatever they said would be private for now.

"I don't feel like talking," Brayden said and took another sip. Maybe if he just kept drinking, they'd leave him alone. He'd kept his secret for longer than Tyler or Matt had kept theirs. He didn't feel like sharing it now, even though he knew the weight of secrets pushed down on them all. Time moved forward, and new people were entering their tight-knit group, changing the dynamics beyond a mere brotherhood.

"You don't have a choice right now," Jackson said smoothly, and then he took another sip. "You see, we know you've been hiding something, but we've let you keep it secret since you don't seem to be in pain. However, things are changing. Ever since Greg died, you've been acting differently. Like you're waiting on something that could actually happen now, instead of watching from the sidelines."

Brayden held back a wince at the bastard's name, even though Jackson wasn't that far off.

"That brings us to the second reason we're here," Tyler said. "All of this comes back to Allison, and we're going to talk about that. Deal?"

"Since when did we become a group of women who talk about our feelings?" Brayden asked.

"Since always, you ass. We talk more than most, so get over yourself," Jackson scolded.

Brayden drained the last of his beer and signaled to cut himself off. He needed to drive later, and he didn't need to drown himself in liquid courage.

"Where do you want me to start?" Brayden asked, resigned.

"How about with the coin around your neck? Come on. We've been asking for years; you've been avoiding for years. Based on everything that's been happening in the past few months, it's time to spill. What are we in for here?" Tyler asked.

"It's my lucky coin."

Jackson blinked. "And? That really doesn't tell us anything. Plenty of people have lucky coins, yet yours seems different. And considering this is Holiday, where all things holiday and paranormal seem to be collected, and the fact we're Coopers and can't seem to get away from the blasted things, that can't just be a lucky coin."

The anger and bitterness when Jackson talked about holidays and paranormals surprised Brayden. Considering Jackson wasn't a fan of change, it made sense that he hadn't liked how their family had been turned upside down in recent months.

"I'm a lucky man," Brayden explained. At his brothers' stares, he continued, "I've always been lucky. At least since I was five and I found the end of a rainbow."

Tyler and Jackson's eyes widened, and Brayden chuckled.

"Yes, an actual rainbow."

"But, you can't find the end of one," Jackson said. "Rainbows are just refracted light like a prism. The position changes as you change your position. That's the whole point of your eyes and perception."

Brayden loved when his dentist and science-driven brother got technical.

"Sometimes, Jacks, the science of it all gets skewed when magic enters the fray."

Jackson cursed. "This is why I miss things the way they were."

Tyler frowned. "I don't, not really. It's because of magic that I got Abigail and Matt got Jordan and Justin got Rina. I don't think I could give up the magic in exchange for losing any of that. Not even a little bit."

Jackson rolled his eyes. "If you all had been meant to get together, then you would have. Magic shouldn't have been a part of it. That's beside the point. Ignore me and my old man crankiness."

"Always do," Tyler said. "So, Brayden, you found the end of a rainbow. And you say you're lucky...so are you a leprechaun?"

Any other time and place, or any other family, that question would either have been a joke or one that would have landed any one of them in the loony bin, but not in Holiday, not anymore.

"No, but I met one."

"So, what did he look like? I know elves aren't short little people, but what about him?" Tyler asked, excitement on his voice.

Who knew his tough sheriff brother would be so excited about all this?

"He looked like a cranky old man hording his pot of gold. He told me that only a lucky few are destined to find the end of a rainbow. And, because I was special, I got a coin that would prove me lucky."

"You know, any other time, that old man would seem a bit creepy," Jackson said. "I mean, an old man drawing in a little boy with a promise of trinkets?"

"Way to make it gross, you idiot," Brayden said and threw a peanut at him.

"What? I wouldn't want my kids finding old men in fields or wherever the hell you were."

"Oh shut the fuck up," Brayden said and ground his teeth.

"I still have no idea why people think you're the nice one," Tyler said.

"Because I *am* fucking nice. Now are you going to let me finish my story? Or are we going to let Jackson taint a memory for me?"

"I'm just telling you the truth," Jackson answered. "But, do continue."

"Thank you," Brayden said shortly. "He gave me a coin because he said it was my destiny."

Jackson rolled his eyes, and Tyler chucked.

"Sorry," Tyler said. "I'm just laughing at our idiot brother who's so opposed to magic that it's going to be funny as hell when it happens to him."

"Who said it will?" Jackson asked, anger lacing in his tone.

"Because we're Coopers, and that's what happens," Brayden explained. "Now can I finish my fucking story, or are we just going to harp on Jackson some more? Because if it's the latter, I'll just go home. I didn't want to share my story anyway, but it seemed like the right time. It's looking like I was wrong, considering you two don't seem ready. Maybe I'll just tell Matt and Justin."

Tyler held up his hands. "No, sorry. We'll behave. And we'll tell Matt and Justin for you later. That way you don't have to tell the story again. We would have just called Matt and Justin to join us, but they're out with the girls on a double date."

"You just want to hear it first so you'll win or whatever."

"Damn straight." Tyler smiled and drained the last of his beer.

"So despite the fact that he said *destiny*, I still took the coin because it looked cool. Then the next day, I won spelling bingo and a new bike."

Tyler's eyes widened. "I remember you telling me the story of how you won. Considering I wasn't even born yet when you got the coin, that's kind of cool."

"I was two grades higher than you and jealous as hell that you won. Was it because of luck then?" Jackson asked.

"Well, that and skill. But, the luck started then. Ever since, I've won things, been lucky in my deals, had another sense of what to do with my life, where to put my stocks, and other things. I mean, luck doesn't mean good, you know? It could also be bad, so I had to weigh my options. Yeah, people think the definition of luck is a good thing, but there's such a thing as bad luck. So bad that it can roll on top of itself and never let go. So far, I've been lucky in the good sense."

He knocked on the wooden table then traced his coin again, a habit of his that he'd kept from his brothers most of his life.

"Bray, that's awesome," Tyler said in awe. "I just always thought you were good at what you do. And, yeah, luck came to mind, but not the magical kind.

"Well, sure. That's why I have everything I could ever want, right? I have the nice house, a business I love, money rolling in from my investments, and so much more. I'm lucky."

His voice sounded hollow even to his own ears.

"Then why do you sound like you don't have the one thing you want?" Tyler asked, his gaze too knowing.

"This brings us to Allison," Jackson said, and Brayden flinched.

"I'm not going to talk about her."

"At least your acknowledging the fact that there's a subject having to do with her," Tyler said. "I mean, come on, you've been dancing around and evading that subject for ten years."

Brayden started. They'd known that long?

"Yes, we've known that long," Jackson said. "And no, you didn't say what you thought aloud, but it's written all over your face."

"I don't want to talk about her, okay?"

"Why don't you just ask her out?" Tyler asked.

"Because I can't, don't you get that? She doesn't need me." As soon as he voiced the words, he cursed.

He hadn't meant to reveal all that, and now from the stares of his brothers, he wasn't getting off easy.

Crap.

"So you know you have feelings for her?" Jackson asked.

Brayden rolled his eyes. "Are you fucking kidding me? How stupid do you think I am? Of course I know. I know you all thought I'd just been in my own little world and hadn't known what my feelings were, but I knew. I've always known. But, they're my feelings. Not yours. So stay out of it, okay? Ally doesn't need me in her life any more than I already am. Don't mess with it."

He got up and left some cash on the table, leaving his brothers staring at him with looks of astonishment on their faces.

Well, they'd asked after all.

They'd just have to deal with the consequences.

He got in his truck and made it back to his place, a sprawling hillside home with six bedrooms, waiting for a family.

One he was pretty sure he'd never have.

An image of Lacy, Aiden, and Cameron playing in the halls, their laughter echoing like some long-forgotten dream passed over his mind, and Brayden closed his eyes, trying to block out the picture that would never come to pass.

He could only imagine putting the kids to bed then slowing stripping down Allison to nothing but skin, tasting each inch and loving her like no man ever would.

A dream, nothing more.

He hadn't consciously built the place for her and the kids, but he'd done it just the same.

And it was all for nothing.

Because of the coin, he had everything in the world. A home, a job, a dream...everything...

Everything but the one thing that could make him whole.

He had everything in the world but Allison, and that was the problem.

He felt content about life, yet he also felt empty.

He had all the money in the world, yet no one to share it with.

He had no one to talk about his day with.

No one to share his dreams with.

No matter how much money he gave away, making sure others could live and find happiness, he always made more, and it just make him sicker.

There were other things more important than money, even more important than a home and dreams.

There was that one thing he couldn't have, and he couldn't even help her realize she could have more. She didn't take charity beyond what she needed. She was more independent than most because she'd had to be.

All his luck in the world hadn't been able to protect her when she needed him most.

Brayden didn't deserve Allison.

He knew that.

Now he just had his empty house to give him comfort because all the luck in the world couldn't bring Allison to him.

Chapter 3

"Mom!" Cameron yelled from his room. "Aiden is looking at me!"

"So what, buttface?" Aiden yelled back at his brother from the same room, which also happened to be Lacy's room.

The three kids shared the only bedroom while Allison slept in the storage closet that came with the apartment, roughly the size of the cupboard under the stairs that Harry slept in. She didn't need much more.

Sure, keep telling yourself that.

"I'm not a buttface. You're the booger eater," Cameron yelled back.

"Shut up, puke head."

Oh yes, her boys were growing up. Allison resisted the urge to roll her eyes. Even though Aiden was almost a teenager, she swore he reverted to a younger kid when fighting with his brother. Though she couldn't be sure that a teenage boy didn't like a good buttface insult. She'd never lived with one before.

This was why she needed a man around.

No, no. She didn't. Not even a little bit.

"Mom!" Cameron bellowed. "Why aren't you helping? Aiden is *still* looking at me!"

Allison walked the short distance to her kids' room and folded her arms across her chest, giving her best mom-pose.

"I'm just trying to figure out what happened to my nice, growing-up boys. Because from what I'm hearing, they aren't in this room."

Aiden opened his mouth to talk, and Allison held her hand up.

"No, no excuses. I don't want you guys to call each other names. You know that. It's hard enough when you go out and people call each other names and you have to stand up for each other. I don't want you two to act like degenerates and beat down on each other. Do you understand me? You're brothers. Act like you love each other."

"We do love each other, Mom," Aiden said then smiled. "That doesn't mean we *like* each other."

Cameron smiled and nodded. "Yep, that wasn't in the brother contract."

Allison held back a laugh at her boys who were too smart for their own good. "We'll have to add that clause in, shall we?"

Her boys dissolved into fits of laughter, their fighting forgotten. She loved when she didn't have to scold them with more than a few simple words. Bringing her boys to smiles and giggles was so much better than yelling.

Not a bad day for a mom.

"Mommy!" Lacy called from their small kitchen where she was finishing up her cereal.

Okay, maybe she spoke too soon on the whole day thing.

"Coming, dear," she said as she gave her boys a once-over. "Finish putting on your shoes and brush your teeth. We don't want to be late for school."

The boys groaned, even though she knew they both actually enjoyed classes, Aiden more than Cameron. Her kids were going to finish school, go to college, and be something. Something more than her.

She'd finished high school—barely. She'd been pregnant and married by the time that summer rolled around and her friends where leaving for college.

She'd stayed behind with Greg. The man she'd thought would be her center.

God, how much of an idiot could she have been?

She should have been her own freaking center, not some man's.

Allison shook her head and walked back to the kitchen, burying the memory of a time long passed when she'd made foolish choices. Though every time she said that, she wanted to kick herself.

Without those choices, she wouldn't have her babies, so all in all, she'd do it again.

Anything for her kids.

"What is it, Lace?" she asked as she walked into the small kitchen, picking up a dishtowel on her way in, then cleaned out the boys' cereal bowls. She barely even noticed anymore because she cleaned up as she breathed. It was just second nature by this point.

"I want to bring in Brayden for my show and tell. Do you think he'd come?"

Her heart did that annoying little flutter thing at the mention of Brayden's name, and she tamped it down.

"Why would you want to bring in Brayden, dear? I thought you were going to bring in the painting you did?"

She knew why she was fighting off Brayden's influence in her kids' lives, and she mentally hit herself. She needed to rein him back, but she was afraid she'd been too late.

Lacy stuck out her bottom lip and narrowed her eyes. "I don't want to show off a silly painting. I'd rather show off Brayden instead. He plays with cars and helps me with my bike. He has funny stories and makes me smile. He's what I want to show everyone since I don't have a daddy. This way people can't say anything mean again."

Allison broke down right there. Oh, no, not physically, but, mentally, her body shook, and fat tears rolled down her cheeks. She wanted to curse Greg and the world around her.

She knew kids could be mean, and she did her best to stop the bullying, starting with the other parents in town. She'd missed something intrinsically brutal.

Allison knelt down and brushed a lock of hair behind Lacy's ear, swallowing hard as she did so.

"We can ask him. He's a very busy man, but we can ask." Lacy's face brightened, but Allison didn't pull her into a hug yet. "I want to know who said those things, Lace. I know you miss your daddy, but that doesn't give the other kids an excuse to be mean."

Allison had always had to tiptoe the line involving Greg in her children's eyes. As much as she'd hated him, though she knew she couldn't hide everything, especially not from Aiden, her kids had needed a father.

"I'm okay, Mommy. I have Aiden and Cameron, who watch my back." Allison held back a smile at the words that came from her little girl that sounded so much like her boys. "Plus, when I bring in Brayden, I'll get to show him off."

Allison smiled, imagining Lacy showing off her Brayden.

She had to remember that, as much as she wanted to be selfish and block Brayden from their lives, he was good for them. Even if it hurt her beyond measure to think of him moving on.

Allison pulled Lacy into her arms for a moment, inhaling her sweet just-a-little-girl smell, then pulled back.

"Okay, go brush your teeth, and then let's get on the road, kiddo."

Lacy smiled and rushed to the small bathroom they all shared. Allison did some last minute cleaning, grabbed her apron for work, and put on her coat.

"Come on, you guys, let's get going."

The three kids piled into their coats, Allison helping Lacy zip hers, and put on their backpacks, and they were on their way.

Her car was still in the shop, but it would only be a short walk for them.

"Brayden!" Lacy called and let go of Allison's hand, running to Brayden, who held his arms out for her as she jumped.

"Good morning, Lace," he drawled in that deep voice of his.

"Mommy said I could bring you for show and tell. So now I get to show you off."

"Get," Allison corrected and blushed. She always seemed to be blushing around this man.

"Get," Lacy repeated and kissed Brayden's cheek.

He grinned then rubbed his cheek against hers. "That sounds like a plan, Lace. Just let me know when, and I'll get there. Now, how about I get you three to school and your momma to work?"

Allison shook her head, trying to tamp down on the warmth that spread through her at his nearness.

"It's not that far a walk, Brayden. We should be fine." Even as she said it, she knew it was a lost cause. Her boys had already bumped fists with the man and were climbing into the truck while Lacy had wrapped her arms around Brayden's neck, daring Allison to say no.

"It's not a big deal. I just wanted to make sure you guys were safe."

Well, she knew when she'd lost.

Stupid, happy, lovey-dovey feelings and all that crap.

"Well, all I can say is thank you I guess," she conceded, and Brayden grinned.

The damn grin was creating all that stupid warm and tingly crap inside her.

"I still have Lacy's booster in the backseat, so just hop in the front and we're ready to go."

Allison nodded and climbed in, too aware of the heat radiating from Brayden as he did the same.

She could do this. It wasn't as if she'd jump his bones right there.

Great, now that mental image wouldn't go away.

And what a nice image that was.

They dropped the kids off first, all three of them hugging Brayden and her on their way out. The whole situation reeked of domestic bliss, and just for a moment, she could imagine what it would be like if this were a real family outing with a man who really loved her.

And then the moment shattered with its inevitable fragility as she spotted some of the other mothers eyeing Brayden's truck with a mixture of envy and a curiosity that would lead to more gossip.

Justin, the school principle, and Abby, one of the teachers, waved, and Brayden and Allison waved back.

"Let's get you to work," Brayden said, his voice gruff.

"Thanks."

As he drove, she watched as he took a deep breath. "I'm sorry. I didn't think of what everyone's reaction to me dropping you off would be. I don't want them to think that you're staying with me for anything more than just as a friend."

She shrugged. It was too late to have regrets. "It's Holiday; they need gossip. It's not like it's wrong anyway if we were together. It's not like either of us are married or with someone. People just need to grow up and get over it. I just hope the other kids leave my kids alone."

Brayden nodded. "I hope so too. I don't like the thought of your kids being hurt."

And right there. That was why she loved him.

Yep, she totally loved the man she'd never have.

That was just par for the course in her life.

Brayden parked in front of the diner and got out with her.

"Don't you have to go to work?" she asked, secretly pleased he was coming in.

"I need my morning cup of coffee." He grinned. "I thought you'd be used to it by now."

She shook her head and chucked. He'd been doing the same thing every day for years; she should have remembered. Apparently being in close proximity to the man had taken away her mental capacity.

They went in, and she set him up with a cup of coffee and got ready for her shift. When she walked past the counter though, she froze.

Greg.

No, that couldn't be right. Greg was dead, but why was the spitting image of him standing next to Brayden?

Her gaze rested on Brayden's as her body shook and she felt the blood leave her face. She saw the surprise and confusion in Brayden's eyes that surely matched her own.

No, not Greg. He couldn't be back.

Brayden reached out and grabbed her by the waist, letting her body rest against his, as a curse let out under his breath. She swallowed hard, taking in his heat and strength.

Damn her for being weak.

She strengthened, but let Brayden's arm stay wrapped around her waist. She needed the comfort, if only for a moment.

"Who...who are you?"

The man with Greg's face tilted his head. "I see you recognize me, Allison Malone."

"Stop playing games. Why are you here?" Brayden said, his normally smooth tone deep with anger.

She'd curse herself later for it, but she was glad he was there with her in the empty diner. She needed him.

"I wasn't talking to you." He turned to Allison. "I'm David, Greg's brother, and I'm here to give you a warning."

No. No, this couldn't be happening. She'd hidden from Greg's family for so long because of the horror stories he'd told her about them. If they scared Greg, the scariest man in her life, she hadn't wanted a moment with them.

"What warning?" Brayden asked.

"Like I said, I wasn't talking to you," David repeated.

Thank God he was here because she couldn't speak. Thoughts where running wild in her head.

How fast could she get out of here and get her babies?

What did this man want?

Where were his parents?

Would he hurt her like Greg had?

David smiled, a truly feral smile that sent a shudder through Allison. "I'm here for your children. They're of our blood, our family. We don't want them raised by a whore like you."

Before she could blink, Brayden had the man by the throat and pinned against the wall.

"Watch your fucking mouth around her. Do you understand me? You say another thing like that, and I'll fucking kill you. Got it?"

Though she'd lost the strength of Brayden's embrace, Allison straightened, trying to look strong, as though she could take anything down in her path.

She didn't want to be weak.

Not anymore.

David only smiled again. "You're nothing, but I see that she's opened her legs again. Not a surprise there."

Brayden punched David in the face, the sound of bones breaking echoing in Allison's head.

David screamed, holding his nose. "Oh you're going to pay for that, dick." With that, he left the diner, passing Rina as she walked in. The two looked at each other and froze for a moment before David walked away.

Rina came in and rushed to Allison's side. "Oh, my God, what happened? Why was that man here? Brayden, go in the back and put ice on that hand. Allison, sit down, you're as a pale as a ghost."

The little elf shuffled everyone around, and Allison did as she was told.

"I need to go get my kids," she said, her voice hollow.

"I'm calling Justin now to keep an eye on them," Brayden said as he came out with ice in one hand and his phone in the other. "We'll go get them in a second."

She nodded and drank the rest of Brayden's coffee, needing strength.

"Now, how did you know that man?" Rina asked.

"He's Greg, my late husband's twin brother."

Rina's eyes widened, and she paled. "Oh, my God."

"What? What's wrong?"

Rina looked around the empty diner, and Allison thanked God it was the lull before the rush when another waitress would come in.

"That man? He's a gnome. He's not human Ally. They make you do things you don't want to do."

There was a buzzing in her ears as Allison tried to process that information.

Not human?

That would mean Greg wasn't human.

And her babies.

She blinked a couple times, trying to get those black spots out from her field of vision. She would *not* faint like a damsel in distress.

Brayden came up behind her and let her rest against his chest as she tried to breathe.

"A gnome?" she asked, barely able to comprehend.

Rina nodded, but didn't say anything more as Rachel, Allison's co-worker, walked in.

"What's wrong, guys?" Rachel asked as she took off her coat.

Allison stood up, Brayden on her heels, his hand in the small of her back. Rachel's eyes glanced toward the gesture, and a smirk crossed her face.

Great, that news would be around town in ten minutes. Whatever. Who cared about gossip when her babies could be in danger?

"I need to go pick up my kids. Can you cover my shift?"

Rachel's eyebrows rose at the suggestion. Usually, Allison would never leave her shift when she so desperately needed the money, but this wasn't a normal case.

Rachel shrugged. "Sure, whatever."

"Thank you," Allison said as she ran to the back and grabbed her things.

They hurried to the parking lot, and Rina touched her arm. "Get your kids and go home. I'll meet you there, okay?"

Allison nodded, and Brayden rubbed small circles in her back. God, she needed his strength right now. As much as she wanted to be super-mom and do everything on her own, she knew when to stop worrying by herself and ask for help.

They climbed into Brayden's truck, and she wrung her hands. "You need to be at work, Bray."

He looked at her as though she'd gone crazy and grabbed her hand and squeezed. "I have guys to run it for me. You and those kids are more important."

Yes, she loved this man.

He cleared his throat and took his hand back. She held back a sigh at the loss of contact.

Damn it.

"When I told Justin a little of what was going on, he pulled your kids out of class so they're hanging out in his office with him. They're not alone, Ally, okay?"

She nodded, instantly relieved even though she needed to see them to be sure.

When they pulled in and got to Justin's office, her kids ran up to her, confused.

"What's wrong, Mom?" Aiden asked.

"We just need to take you home, okay?"

Oh, God, how was she going to explain this to them?

Justin gave them a look, but Brayden shook his head. "I can explain later," he said, and Justin nodded.

She bundled her babies up, and Brayden drove them to her apartment. Rina sat in her car in the parking lot and joined them in Allison's too-small living room.

Her kids looked scared, confused, and lost. Lacy climbed up into Brayden's lap and curled into a ball as he ran a hand through her hair and down her back. Allison sank into the couch next to him as her boys sat on either side of them, their fear adding to hers.

Rina sat in the chair across from them and tried to smile.

"What happened, Mom?" Aiden asked.

As much as she wanted to lie and tell them nothing, she knew the more knowledge they had, the safer they'd be. Even if it would scare them.

"A man came into the diner today," she began. "Remember when Daddy told you about his family and how things were different with them?"

And, boy, howdy, were they different.

They nodded, and Aiden snuggled into her side.

"You know how I'm an elf, guys, right?" Rina said into the silence, and Allison was grateful. She honestly didn't know how to start.

"You work for Santa," Lacy said, a smile on her face.

Rina grinned back and nodded. "Yep, I work for Santa. I know you know elves are real, but we're not the only beings with pointy ears."

Allison tensed, and Brayden patted her thigh. She tried to ignore the warmth that spread through her at his touch. This wasn't exactly the perfect time to entertain those thoughts.

"You see, we elves have cousins called gnomes," Rina continued.

The kids gasped, and Allison shot a look at Brayden. Was this really happening? Allison caught Rina's glance, and she knew there was more to the story than what Rina was saying, but couldn't reveal in front of the kids.

"Like the one with the red hat?" Cameron asked.

Rina grinned. "Sort of. The thing is, gnomes look just like humans except they have pointed ears like elves and aren't as short as elves. They also can have black eyes if they do darker magic, but like elves, can hide their appearance. Ally, you wouldn't have seen Greg in his natural state if he hadn't wanted you to see it. They also have magic, but only full-blooded gnomes have pure magic."

Allison held her breath. Her babies didn't look like what Rina described. She'd seen every part of them and had wiped their little butts and cleaned their runny noses. She would have noticed something like a pointy ear or magic.

They were only half-blooded. That had to count for something.

"What does this have to do with why you took us out of school, Mom? And why were you talking about Dad's family?" Aiden asked, his eyes cloudy with confusion.

Allison squeezed Aiden's hand and turned so she could see her other two children. "Because apparently your father was a gnome."

Lacy's eyes filled, and Brayden squeezed her close as Cameron shifted so he too sat on Brayden's lap. Aiden tapped her on the shoulder and blinked.

"But...but he never said anything," her eldest son stuttered.

"I know, baby. I don't understand either, but his brother came into the diner today, and Rina recognized him as a gnome."

"I don't want to be a gnome," Cameron said as he patted Lacy's back.

"We're only half gnomes," Aiden corrected and laid his head on Allison's shoulder.

"That means you probably won't have the pointy ears or magic," Rina reassured. "We won't know until puberty, but I don't think it will be a problem."

"But, we're different," Aiden stated.

"So? We're all different," Brayden said as he soothed Lacy's tears. "Who wants to be like anyone else? And no matter what, you still have your mom. And me. And all of the Coopers."

Cameron nodded and leaned into his hold.

Thank God Brayden was there.

She'd found herself saying that a lot lately.

"Wait, why was Dad's brother here?" Aiden asked after Lacy had calmed down. "I thought they weren't nice people and we should stay away."

Allison gave a small smile and tried to look reassuring. "I know. That's why we pulled you out of school. The man's name is David, and he's your father's twin." She looked at her children as they absorbed that tidbit of information. "If you see a man that looks like your dad, you run, okay? He's not a nice man."

It hurt her to say things like that, to bring fear into her children's lives. Greg's family wasn't to be messed with, not when his brother had so blatantly told her he was there for her kids.

"Why would Daddy's family want to hurt us?" Lacy asked.

Allison swallowed hard. Damn Greg and his family for bringing this into her family. "I don't know, pumpkin. Sometimes people don't do nice things, but no matter what, you have to remember that I will always be here for you. I won't let them take you."

"Take us?" Cameron asked.

She silently cursed herself for letting that slip, but it was important that they knew not to go anywhere with their...uncle. God, she hated the fact that he was of their blood.

"I want you three to be careful and stick together. I can't keep you from school for long, but until we make a plan, I don't want you three alone."

She knew she hadn't answered the question, but it was the best she could do.

"I know it's scary, but you're not alone," Brayden reassured, and she fell that much more in love with him.

Greg's family wanted her children, but they weren't going to get them. She might only have a high school education, but she had a job, and her kids had a roof over her head. They couldn't take away her babies without a fight.

Legally, she didn't even think they had a case, but in terms of magical beings, she didn't think that was an issue. If the gnomes planned anything to harm her children, they'd have to come through her.

The kids went to the other room and Rina sat across from her, a frown on her face. "Ally, I don't know exactly what happened in your marriage, but he could have made you stay against your will. Do you understand that? It wasn't your fault."

Her vision blackened at the words.

No, she couldn't think about that. Not yet.

She needed to think of her children.

Her gaze met Brayden's, and he gave her a nod.

And she wouldn't be alone. No, she had someone to stand by her side, at least for a little while.

Together, maybe they had a chance.

Chapter 4

Allison woke as tension filled her body. Something was off. It was still dark outside, and she looked at the clock, realizing she'd been asleep for only an hour.

After Rina had explained a bit more about elves and gnomes, she'd left so she could tell the Coopers what was going on and to keep everyone updated. Brayden had stayed for the rest of the day, completely ignoring his responsibilities, and ate dinner with them. When he would have stayed and slept on her very small couch, she forced him to leave.

Tyler, the town sheriff, had promised to have his deputies drive by every hour, and she had the windows and doors locked. She knew it wasn't the safest place, but she couldn't keep

Brayden away from his life and in her tiny apartment forever.

Even if she wanted to.

Well then, she needed to stop thinking about what she felt about them because it wasn't as important as her children's safety.

She could be a woman later; she had to be a mom now.

That tension increased along her spine, and she sat up in her bed, trying to listen for any off sound. She could hear only the clock ticking in the kitchen, the slight sound of Cameron's snoring, and the wind as it brushed against the windows.

Something wasn't right. Call it a mom thing, but she couldn't sleep not knowing what had woken her up.

Allison crept out of bed, grabbing her cell phone in the process. Hopefully, it was just her hyper-aware nerves playing tricks on her senses and not someone trying to get into her home.

She shuddered at the thought.

The apartment had cooled down as the sun had set, and she cursed her flaky landlord and his lack of repair skills. The heat may have been on, but it wasn't doing its job. Thankfully, she owned numerous blankets and quilts to keep them all warm, but it was getting ridiculous.

She knew she was thinking about other things rather than what could be happening as a defense mechanism, but she couldn't help it. She didn't want there to be anything wrong.

Allison looked into her kids' room and saw only her sleeping babies, nothing else. Relief slid through her even as she told herself not to get her hopes up.

She tiptoed to the living room and didn't see anything out of the ordinary there, or in her small kitchen.

Maybe it was just in her mind.

Allison walked past the front door, made sure it was locked, and started back to her room. The hairs on the back of her neck rose, and the door crashed open behind her. She turned on her heel, arms raised as the moon shined on David as he raised a knife and slashed through her forearm.

She screamed in pain, clutching her arm, and fell to the ground when he pushed her. Blood poured from the wound as she bit her tongue trying not to cry. Every breath tore at her skin, sending glass shards of pain through her.

"I told you I'd come for them."

"You can't have my children," she said, her voice sounding firmer than she expected.

"I don't really care what you think you can do." He started toward the bedroom, and she kicked out, tripping him.

He lashed out, hitting her twice as hard.

Allison screamed, feeling along the floor to where she'd dropped her phone then dialed 911. She sat up, her body aching. Before she could speak, David pulled at her leg, spilling her back onto the floor with a crash, her head thumping painfully. She swallowed back the bile that rose in her throat as he slapped at her, over and over again.

She shielded her face and held her arm. If he kept his attention on her, then he wouldn't be near her kids. Hopefully her kids would run. That's what she had told them to do.

"Get off my mom!" Cameron yelled as he jumped on David's back.

Allison's heart fell down to her stomach at the sight of David throwing Cameron against the wall, her little baby slumping to the floor and cradling his arm as tears ran down his cheeks.

"Cameron!" she yelled as she staggered to her feet. Blood streamed from her arm, and her body ached in every place David had hit her, but she barely felt it. Her baby was hurt, and this bastard deserved to die.

Sirens echoed through her apartment as the police grew close. David cursed and slapped her again, knocking her into the couch as she went to Cameron's side. David ran out the door, leaving them alone as the adrenaline pulsed through her system.

"Mom?" Aiden called as he hurried toward them, Lacy clutched to his side.

"Come here."

Lacy knelt beside Cameron, her cheeks wet with tears and her eyes wide.

Cameron was pale, and he couldn't stop crying. She looked at his arm and wanted to throw up. It was bent at an odd angle and had to hurt even more than the cut on hers.

"Baby?"

"Mommy, it hurts," he cried, and she wanted to find David and kill him. Slowly. Nobody hurt her babies.

"Allison?" Tyler called from the doorway. "Dear God." He called over his shoulder for the paramedics as cops filled her apartment.

"He's gone," she whispered, her voice not strong enough to talk any louder.

She hadn't thought it was real, not really. Yes, she'd taken the threat to her children's safety seriously, but deep down, she had hoped David was all bark, no bite.

Oh, how she'd been wrong.

Tyler kneeled down. "I'll take care of it. We're going to take care of you. As for the reports, we can leave things out, okay?"

She knew he was saying that for the benefit of the children when, at any other time, talk of reports when she was bleeding and her son's arm was broken wouldn't have been the best time. There were some things, like magical beings, that couldn't go in reports.

"Ally?" Brayden called as he ran through the door. His hair looked disheveled, his jacket undone, and his clothes looked thrown on. His eyes were bright, his body taut, his fists clenched.

Lacy wiggled from Allison's side and ran to his open arms. He held her close, and Allison watched as he closed his eyes and stood there with her daughter in his arms like a father who'd almost lost his child.

She didn't have time to think about how she felt about that. Her arm hurt as though she was dying, and her son was in pain.

Her feelings would have to wait.

Aiden helped her stand as the paramedics came and began to treat both her and Cameron, insisting they would also need to go to the hospital for further treatment. Even though the costs would be scary as hell, there was no question of its necessity.

Aiden gripped her hand, and she held him close.

"Bray," she whispered, and he came closer to her, Lacy in his arms. "Can you watch Aiden and Lacy while they look at my arm please?" Her voice shook, and she knew if she didn't let them give her something for the pain, she'd break down and sob right there.

"Anything you need," he said, he voice strained as though he was holding something back.

Aiden held onto her hand for dear life, but he slid under Brayden's arm.

"Ma'am?" The female paramedic had finished bandaging her arm up, but Allison knew it wasn't over. "We're going to take your son in the ambulance because we're afraid he hit his head and he needs to get to the hospital to get his arm set. Though I know you'll want to be with him, I need you to come with him because this wound is going to need stitches."

She nodded, not surprised. "Is Cameron going to be okay?"

The woman gave a reassuring smile. "Your little boy is very brave. He's going to be fine, but we need to get to the hospital soon in any case. I'm worried about the cut you have."

She nodded and looked for Brayden, needing to make sure he'd take care of things.

"Don't worry, Ally. I'll take Aiden and Lacy with me in my truck and we'll meet you two at the hospital. They won't leave my sight. You can trust me."

"You know I do."

His eyes flickered, but he didn't say anything, merely nodded.

"Be good for Brayden," she said as the paramedics led her and Cameron to the doors of the ambulance.

"I'm scared, Mommy," Lacy said as she sucked on her thumb, a habit that she'd long since given up.

Greg's brother had taken more than just a night away from her family. He'd taken their security and so much more by breaking into their home and hurting her and Cameron.

Allison didn't know how she was going to fix that—how she *could* fix that. However, though her mind wanted to run in a thousand different directions, she first needed to focus on her son. Then she could make a list and plans for everything else. One step at a time while planning for a hundred.

That was her mom motto.

Her hands shook as she took Cameron's tiny one. He looked up at her with his big green eyes and tried to smile.

"Hey, brave boy, we're going to make you all better." Her voice trembled, but she smiled back.

"They said I'd get a cast. Can I get it in green? And will everyone sign it? Even Brayden?"

Brayden again. It seemed he was tangled in their lives on every level he could get but hers. Something that wouldn't change—couldn't change.

"Let's see what colors they have first, but if they have green, I don't see why not." She took a deep breath at the thought that he even needed a cast. "And we'll all sign it, even Brayden."

His lips trembled as tears slid down his face. The paramedic was at Cameron's side, checking his vitals and then her arm, but she could at least hold her baby's hand and squeeze.

"I know it hurts, Cam, but we'll get you better soon."

"I'm sorry, Mommy."

There was that Mommy again. She was only that when he was scared or in trouble. As much as she loved to be Mommy again, she hated the thought of Cameron so scared.

"We'll talk later about what you did." She couldn't bear to think of it at the moment.

"But, he was hurting you like Daddy used to. I didn't want you to get hurt anymore. I'm sorry I jumped on that man and you."

The paramedic's sharp eyes met hers, and she raised her chin. Yes, she'd stayed with a man who beat her. She still didn't know why, but that was her cross to bear.

And her children's.

Something she'd never forgive herself for.

Allison looked into her son's eyes and prayed that the shadows that lurked would fade away, leaving only the innocence of a boy who wanted his mom. Though things were never that easy.

"You should have done what I asked and stayed with Aiden. As much as I love that you stood up for yourself and me, I don't want you hurt. Okay?" Cameron nodded. "We'll talk more later."

The ambulance stopped, and the back door opened. She kissed Cameron's hand and climbed out, letting the doctors and nurses take her through the Emergency Room doors as she watched them do the same to her son.

"Ally."

She turned and saw Brayden walk through the doors, Lacy in his arms and Aiden holding his hand. The corners of her mouth lifted in a weak smile as some of the pressure on her heart lifted.

Brayden would take care of them while she got her stitches and Cameron's bone could be set. At least she could count on him for that.

Seventeen stitches later, with a list of instructions on how to care for the wound, she had to sit in the waiting room with the entire Cooper clan—minus Tyler—while Cameron went to get a X-ray. She would rather have been back there with him, but she knew he was in safe hands. Tyler had gone back with him since she had been getting fixed herself at the time.

Allison slid into the seat beside Brayden and wrapped her uninjured arm around Aiden.

"You did so good, you know that?" She kissed the top of his head and held him hard. "You took care of your sister and made sure she was okay. I'm so proud of you."

He looked up at her with dried tears on his cheeks. "But, I let Cameron get hurt."

She kissed his forehead and brushed his shaggy hair from his face. "No, David hurt Cameron, not you. You can't control everything your brother and sister do. I know Cam shouldn't have done what he did, but you took care of Lacy, so I'm proud of you. Do you understand?"

He nodded and laid his head on her shoulder, his breath ragged.

Allison looked over at Lacy in a deep sleep, her little cherub face on Brayden's chest. Thank God Lace could sleep after what she'd just seen. Allison wasn't sure she would be able to herself.

"Thank you," she said to Bray, her eyes on his.

"You shouldn't have to thank me," he grumbled. "This shouldn't have happened to begin with."

The vehemence in his voice surprised her and brought her hand to his arm. "I know. I want to hurt him too."

Brayden breathed out through his nose, as if trying to rein in his temper, and shook his head. "You're not going back to your place."

She frowned and looked at the other Coopers in the room. The men looked as though they were ready to punch something while the women looked like they'd be right at their heels.

Allison felt overwhelmed at all the support in the room and the fact that these people treated her like family, even though she knew she wasn't.

"Mrs. Malone?" the doctor asked as he walked into the room. She stood quickly, Aiden by her side, and the rest of the Coopers joined her, though Brayden sat where he was, Lacy still asleep in his lap.

"That's me. Is he okay? Can I see him now?"

"Cameron is going to be fine, it's a compound break of his radius, and since he's still growing, it will heal quickly. He'll just need to rest a bit."

Even though the idea of a broken bone scared her, relief poured through her, and her knees felt weak. Jackson held her by the waist, keeping her up, and she could have sworn she heard a growl coming from Brayden's direction, but she couldn't be sure.

A nurse wheeled Cameron out from the door behind the doctor, and Allison rushed to him, hugging him as tight as she could without breaking either of them.

"It's green!" Cameron pumped his unbroken arm and smiled, though his eyes looked a bit loopy from the pain and drugs.

Apparently, all it took was the color cast they wanted and kids bounced back.

The doctor gave yet another list of instructions, leaving Allison, her children, and the Coopers alone in the waiting room.

"You're staying with me," Brayden ordered in the silence.

She raised a brow at his tone. "Excuse me?"

"Good going," Matt coughed, and Jordan elbowed him in the stomach.

Brayden narrowed his eyes on Matt and stood with a sleeping Lacy in his arms. "The door to your place is broken, and it isn't safe. I have tons of room, and I want you to stay with me." He waited a beat. "Please."

Staying with the man she was attracted to? So not a good idea, but she didn't want to be alone, not when she needed help to make sure her kids were safe. God that grated on her.

"I don't take kindly to orders," she said evenly, knowing her children and the Coopers were watching their every movement.

"I'm sorry. I should have said it differently. But, please," he pleaded.

Allison could get over the fact that she was staying with a man she wanted; she had to. She had her kids to think about.

She let out a breath. "Fine, but I don't want to inconvenience you."

"You won't."

Cameron hugged her hard and kissed her arm. "We'll be okay, Mom. Brayden's cool."

Aiden smiled and hugged her other side. "And his house is big, so we'll have room."

God, kid, hit me where it hurts. She knew she didn't have enough to keep them happy, but it hurt to have it thrown in her face.

Brayden took Aiden by the shoulder and frowned as if he knew what she was thinking. It was disconcerting, like they were a real family and he was her other half, her support...her anchor.

Rina came up to them and ruffled Cameron's hair. "We can go and get your things for you. How about you guys just go to Bray's and get some sleep? It's late."

"Thank you, but we can do it."

Jackson shook his head. "No, we can handle it. I know you don't want people pawing through your things, but you need rest. Between the women and us, we should be able to get you what you need. And if we don't, we'll get it later."

Allison shrugged, knowing she was beaten. "Thank you."

"No problem, hon," Justin said as he kissed her cheek.

That started the procession of the Coopers, leaving her and her kids alone in the room with Brayden.

"Let's head out now. It's been a long day."

"I need to take care of the billing first," she said, her head aching even thinking about the cost.

"It's taken care of."

She froze, anger rising. "Excuse me?"

"We'll talk about it later, okay?" He nodded toward the kids, and she lifted her chin.

Oh, they'd be talking about it later.

They made their way to his place, and she stared at it in awe. She'd seen it before, known how large the home was, but now that she was going to stay there, it made her feel small, like her little place wasn't good enough. She knew that wasn't Brayden's intention, but it's what happened anyway.

They got the kids settled in one of the guest rooms as they all wanted to stay together, not quite trying to mask their fears. She and Brayden tucked them in and let them sleep, even though the sun would be rising any moment.

It was a little too domestic for her taste, but she'd push through.

Brayden showed her where she would be sleeping, a room in between the master bedroom and the guest room where the kids were staying.

They both stood in the doorway, shuffling from foot to foot.

"Thank you," she whispered.

"We have a lot to talk about, but, Ally, I won't let anything happen to you and the kids."

She desperately wanted to believe that, but she knew just because someone said it, didn't make it true.

Without warning, he framed her face and lowered his lips to hers. He tasted of coffee and mint, like Brayden. Before she could lean in and let the brush of lips turn into more, he pulled back.

"I'll take care of you," he whispered.

"I don't need taken care of. I just need a place to rest."

He nodded, understanding in his eyes. "I'll see you when we wake up."

He left her in the doorway, her body warm from his touch, yet cooling with the fear that came with it.

They had too much to talk about, too much in their way.

It wasn't the time for feelings and relationships. David could be back at any moment, and her kids were her first priority. Always.

When she laid her head on her pillow, it wasn't her children or David that filled her thoughts. No, it was the touch of soft lips and the promise that came with it.

Chapter 5

"Do you want syrup with your pancakes? Or jelly?" Brayden asked as he dished out breakfast to the three hungry children at the table in his breakfast nook.

"Gross, jelly? Who puts jelly on pancakes? That's just for toast."

Lacy giggled and gently touched Cameron's green cast and Cam shifted, so he could show it off.

Apparently having it broken in a fit of rage from an intruder didn't faze him a bit. No, the kid only cared about the fact that he had the totally cool new green cast for all of his friends to sign.

Brayden vaguely remembered being that age.

"I want a pool of syrup," Lacy explained as she tried to take the bottle from him. He pulled back, remembering the syrup fight he'd had with Justin when he'd been younger and the look of horror on his mom's face when she returned to the kitchen after being gone for two minutes at most.

"I'll pour," he said quickly and covered her cakes then did the same to the boys so she wouldn't feel like a little kid.

Aiden seem to understand, but Cameron frowned before he cut into his stack.

The three of them had woken him up that morning by standing by his bedside staring. Not moving, not saying anything, just staring at him.

They were very lucky he recognized them at the last moment or Allison probably would have killed him.

Slowly.

He was also the lucky one in that he'd remembered to wear pants when he went to sleep, knowing there were children in the house.

When Brayden had finally rubbed the sleep out of his eyes, he'd stared up at Aiden and smiled. The three of them had explained they were really hungry, so hungry that their little bellies were hollow and in need of sugar.

So, he'd pulled on a sweatshirt and made them pancakes. Though Justin was the cook in the family, Brayden could work his way around the kitchen and usually enjoyed doing it.

Cooking for three hungry children had been an experience.

Cooking for them while trying to keep them quiet so their mom could sleep?

A little harder.

As he watched them stuff their faces, syrup going everywhere, he thought he hadn't done such a bad job.

The idea of domesticity sat well on his shoulders, as though it should have been there long before this. He just needed Ally in the kitchen, wrapping her arms around his waist while they drank coffee and talked about what they were going to do that day.

He held back a snort. Yeah, that wouldn't be happening anytime soon.

His impulsive kiss last night, though, seemed to be bringing them in the right direction.

Brayden hadn't even thought about his actions before he did it. She'd just looked so freaking scared and in need of something more than just a quick goodbye and a back to watch walk away. So, he'd leaned down and inhaled that light lavender scent that led him to thoughts of sweaty nights and his place between her thighs and in her life.

Brayden couldn't believe she was in his home, sleeping in his bed. Well, not *his* bed, but close enough. It didn't seem real. He'd loved her for so long, knew her better than he knew himself, even though she held herself at arm's length.

"What's going on here?" Allison asked as she shuffled in, the pants he'd let her borrow too big on her frame.

"Brayden made us pancakes," Lacy explained, showing off the partially chewed cakes in her mouth.

"Don't talk with your mouth full, honey," Allison admonished.

"They were hungry." Brayden couldn't stop looking at her. Her auburn hair was disarrayed around her face, tousled as though she'd spent a sweaty night in his bed, not the heavy sleep she'd probably gotten from the adrenaline withdrawal.

"Why didn't you wake me?" she asked as she walked to the coffee pot and fixed herself a cup as if she owned his kitchen.

An idea that held merit with him.

"You needed your sleep, and I wanted to cook breakfast. There's still some batter if you want me to whip you up some pancakes."

She shook her head. "I'm fine with coffee right now. My stomach is a little too light after last night."

He nodded, understanding. Walking into the room and seeing the blood on the floor and the most important people in his life beyond his brothers huddled on the floor had taken a few years off his life.

They stood silently, a slight tension radiating off both of them from the odd scene playing out between them. Whether it was a sexual tension, something more, or a mixture of both, he didn't know. The kids finished eating, and Ally herded them upstairs to get cleaned up.

Rina and Justin had stopped by early in the morning with their things, so at least everything could feel a little more like home. Even if he wanted it to feel even a little bit more than that.

God, he was a goner.

Brayden jumped in the shower then got dressed in well-worn jeans and a dark Henley, ready to get started. He needed to tell Ally what he was, or at least, the luck he had and how he could help. He didn't want any more secrets between them.

Though he knew it would be a risk considering she'd been married to a gnome for years and hadn't known it. He knew she wouldn't trust magic as much as he wanted.

Though it wasn't as if he were a leprechaun—he just happened to carry their luck.

Yes, Bray, that's a fine line right there.

Brayden cleaned up the kitchen, thoughts about Ally, luck, and how to protect her twirling in his head. He was so lost in his mind; he hadn't even noticed Ally standing next to him, freshly showered and sexy as hell in a T-shirt and jeans.

"Thank you, Brayden," she whispered as she stood a foot away from him.

He swallowed hard and quirked a small smile. "You don't have to thank me, Ally."

She shook her head, her still drying hair falling over her shoulders. "Yes, I do. You're letting us take over your house, even though I know you like your privacy."

Brayden folded his arms above his chest, pleased when her eyes dilated while she looked at his forearms. He was half tempted to flex and preen, but he held back.

"I like my privacy from the peeping Toms in Holiday. Everyone is in everyone else's business and I'd rather hang out at home."

"Yet, here we are, invading your home."

"You can't invade something you're welcome to."

"Then why us?"

How did he explain that she was welcome in the home he'd built for the dream of her and her kids being in his life? Even when he thought it he knew it sounded like a stalker, not like a normal person.

"You're part of the family."

Her eyes clouded and he knew he'd said the wrong thing. He'd meant part of *his* family. He knew she'd taken it as part of the Coopers. As if he only did it because he felt obligated, not because he wanted to.

Damn it.

"I see."

"No, you don't." He'd have to tell her about who he was before he explained what he wanted. She deserved that much. "Are the kids upstairs?"

She nodded. "They have school work to do, even though they're not going in today. I feel bad that I've taken them out of school two days in a row, but I just don't trust David not to do something."

"Justin and Abby will be there, and by now the town knows that someone came into your home."

She gave a hollow laugh at that. Yes, the gossip chain of Holiday was alive and well.

"You know they probably already know I'm staying here. I can just imagine what they're saying."

"Who cares? You're protecting your kids. Screw what the others say."

"It doesn't look like I have much choice. Though I still don't feel like I'm protecting my kids just by being in a new place."

"We should talk."

"I don't know if I like the sound of that."

He held out his hand and she cautiously grabbed it. He tried to ignore the soft feel of her skin beneath his but failed. Would she be soft all over?

Brayden looked into her eyes and knew her thoughts had followed the same path as his.

Okay, time to talk about something else or he might just kiss her right there in his kitchen where the kids could come in at any moment, causing a whole new set of problems.

He brought her to his office, the place where he read by the fire or worked on things for his shop. The shop he hadn't been to in a couple of days. Thank God for his workers who knew what they were doing.

Brayden watched as she walked along the bookcases, her hand still in his, so he was forced to follow her.

"You have so many books," she said, her fingers tracing along the spine of some of them.

Why did he feel like the Beast while his Beauty found the library?

Maybe that was something better to think about later.

Or not at all.

He shrugged. "I like to read."

"And I thought you were just a mechanic."

For some reason that bugged him. "Really? Just a grease monkey without much else?"

She shook her head, a small smile on her face. "No, but you're very defensive on that. I know you're more than just a man good with his hands."

She blushed beat red and Brayden barely resisted the urge to adjust himself.

Oh, he was good with his hands. He just had to get her to trust him enough to prove it.

"I meant with cars."

"Sure you did."

Ally rolled her eyes and pulled her hand away as if just noticing she'd been holding onto it this whole time. She moved to create more space between them and Brayden let her. She might even want more space once he was done talking to her.

"Okay, so what did you need to tell me? I don't want to leave the kids alone for too long.

Who knows what they'll get into in your house?"

"They'll be fine for a minute."

"I don't think you know them too well if you think that."

Brayden grinned. "Oh, I know what they could do, I'm just choosing to ignore it."

"Good philosophy if you don't want to keep your things nice and unbroken."

He ran a hand through his hair. He was stalling, time to just let it out. "I'm lucky."

Ally blinked. "Uh, okay. Sure. Now what does that have to do with anything?"

He choked out a laugh. "Yeah, that didn't make any sense, did it?"

She shook her head. "Not even a little."

"Okay, when I was a kid, I found a leprechaun." He fingered the coin around his neck, the heat intensifying under his touch. It didn't do that all the time, just during stress and emergencies. Apparently now it knew something big was about to happen.

Her eyes widened. "Like in Lucky Charms?"

"A little. But, the thing is, he gave me this coin. Ever since, I've been lucky. I've been able to use my luck and my own intuition to make more money than I could use, win events, and other things."

"Are you sure it wasn't just you who did all that?"

He looked at her, confused. That thought had never occurred to him. "No, it's the coin. I couldn't be that lucky on my own."

"So you're saying you have magic, but you don't think you could do anything without the coin? That doesn't sound like the confident Brayden I know."

"I tell you I have a little bit of magic, and you turn it around and say I just don't believe in myself enough?"

"No, that's not what I'm saying. Well, okay, maybe I am. But, the thing is, Bray, you could have done any of that stuff without the coin. What makes the thing so special? Maybe it's just in your head, and it's a placebo effect."

He shook his head. "I'm not that good, Ally. Okay, fine, I will admit that I probably could have done some things in my life without the coin, but I sure as hell couldn't have been as good as I am with it around my neck."

"Why don't you try then? Why do you need magic?"

Ah, the heart of the problem. The thing he knew she'd resent or try to run away from.

"First, I can't not use it. The leprechaun said it would always be mine until I found someone to give it to. He said I'd know when the time was right."

She raised a brow and crossed her arms across her chest. "Sounds mysterious."

"Tell me about it. And I haven't given it away yet, never found a reason to."

"Because you like the luck that comes with it?"

"Because it feels like it's mine."

"If you start rubbing it and calling it your 'Precious,' we have a problem, Bray."

He liked the fact that she could at least joke about it, though he didn't know if he liked being compared to 'Gollum' from *Lord of the Rings*.

"The whole point is that, with the luck, I'm a little more equipped to take care of the kids. You wouldn't think so because, hey, it's just luck. Things go good for me, Ally. And, with the coin around my neck, I can feel heat and magic when something bad is going to happen. Plus, I have a kickass security system, Ally."

She puffed her lips out and exhaled. "I don't know, Bray. I don't know if I can deal with this right now. We'll stay here because I feel safer here. I don't know if it's you or just the place, but I'll take your hospitality. Don't get me wrong, I'm grateful, oh, so grateful, but magic scares me."

"I know, Ally."

"No, I don't think you do. I mean, you'd think I'd be okay with magic considering my friends and everything. I don't know, Brayden. Until a day ago, I had no idea that magic had played a role in my life, and now everything is upside down. How can I be sure of anything? Now that I look back on it, I always knew something was off with Greg and our marriage, but I never knew why. I just don't know, Brayden. I lived for years with a gnome, and I didn't know it. I lived with a man who...who did things, and I couldn't leave. I didn't *want* to leave. What does that make me?"

He felt as if someone had shot him, leaving him on the side of the road as he waited for the pain to ebb. What had she been through?

"I'm not ready to talk about it yet, okay? Maybe one day," she said as she turned from him.

Screw leaving them space.

He walked up behind her and wrapped his arms around her waist. "I'm sorry, Ally."

She stiffened then relaxed in his hold. "I'm sorry too."

"Can I tell you something that may make you feel better? Or maybe make you run. I'm not sure."

"What?" she asked as she turned in his arms, her breath warm on his neck.

"I talked to Rina a bit this morning about gnomes when she dropped off your things. She said she'd be back to talk to you later today. She said that gnomes had magic like elves. They can make humans do things, they really try."

Her eyes filled, and she shook her head.

"Whatever happened to you, Ally, it wasn't your fault. If you don't know why you stayed, now we may have a clue. Greg probably forced you."

Anger coursed through him at the thought. He'd kill the bastard if he weren't already dead.

"I hate magic," she whispered, and he held her closer.

"I'm sorry."

They stood there for a bit longer until she pulled away, her face puffy.

"I need to check on the kids. I can't talk about magic right now, okay? But before I go, did you pay my bills, Bray? You said we'd talk about it later... well, it's later."

"Yes, I paid the medical bills, but I don't want you to argue with me about it. I have the money, and the last thing you need right now is the stress of that on your shoulders."

She shook her head. "You had no right. You should have just asked, Bray. I don't like people doing things for me without telling me. Apparently, I had no choice in my life for too long with Greg, and now you're stepping in and doing things for me. I need to stand on my own, don't you see that?"

Brayden stood back, stunned. "You're comparing me to Greg?"

She held up a hand. "Not in the way you think. But, if you want to be in my life, in my kids' lives, then you need to learn to talk to me first. I'm not saying we have a future or anything, but that kiss last night? That we need to talk about."

"Mom!" Aiden called from the other room.

Ally rolled her eyes. "Looks like it's 'mom time'. We'll talk later, okay?" She rose on her tiptoes and let her lips settle on his for a moment. Then, before he could blink, she was gone, and he was alone in his office wondering how the hell he'd gotten there.

What if what she'd said was true? What if all the magic he'd thought he felt was just his imagination?

The coin around his neck warmed, reminding him that it was still there.

No, the magic existed, though the idea that he could be something without it made him feel as though something had clicked into place. Maybe he wasn't just the product of his coin and luck.

Maybe he was something more.

And with Ally, maybe he could *be* something more.

"Brayden?"

He turned and found Lacy in the doorway, her pigtails uneven as she tugged on them.

He smiled and walked toward her so he could lean down to her height. "What is it, squirt?"

"Will you go outside with me and show me the big tree in the backyard?" She batted her little eyelashes at him and tilted her head.

Oh, yeah, this little one had him wrapped around her finger. Brayden found that he didn't care that much. If only Ally knew how much he was wrapped around hers as well.

"Aren't you supposed to be doing your homework?" The last thing he needed was to get Lacy and himself in trouble.

She shook her head, her pigtails twirling. "I already finished mine since I didn't have much. Mommy said we had to go back to school tomorrow, so I want to have fun today. Okay?"

Brayden smiled. Damn, this kid was too cute for her own good. Or was that his own good?

"Let me check with your mom first." He stood up, and she slipped her hands in his.

They walked to the other room where Ally stood over Aiden's shoulder, her body still stiff with the tension of their conversation.

"Is Lacy done with her work?" Brayden interrupted.

Ally looked over her shoulder and smiled. "Yep, though I wish they would have sent more work."

"Brayden's gonna take me outside, Mommy," Lacy announced.

Cameron and Aiden frowned.

"When you two finish, you can come out with us, okay?"

"It's not fair," Cameron mumbled. "She's just a little girl so she doesn't get as much work as me."

"I'm not little!" Lacy yelled.

"Be nice, Cam," Ally said, rolling her eyes. "Thanks, Bray."

Lacy jumped up and down and led Brayden to the back door. He put on their jackets, and they walked hand in hand to the big tree in the back. He kept vigilant though. He didn't trust David not to find them and finish what he started.

"Do you think I can climb it?" Lacy asked.

Brayden looked up at the tree that seemed to get bigger with each breath. An image of Lacy falling and having a cast to match Cam's flashed in his head.

"Maybe not today."

Lacy pouted but didn't say anything, merely kicked the dirt beneath her feet.

Great, he'd disappointed her. He wasn't good at this whole dad thing, considering he wasn't one. But there was one thing he could do to make her smile.

"Hey, Lace, let me show you something."

"What is it?"

"You see this?" He touched the warm coin, and she nodded. "This is a leprechaun's coin."

Her eyes widened. "Really?"

"Yep, I met one when I was little, and now I can do some magic." Okay, he had one trick, but Lacy would love it.

"You mean you're a good magic guy like Justin and not the bad man?"

Brayden pulled her into his arms and kissed her cheek. "Yes, I'm like Justin or Jordan. I'm not like David, okay?"

"So you mean all gnomes are bad?" Her little lip quivered, and Brayden cursed himself.

How had he not thought of this? These kids were half gnomes and hadn't even talked about it. No wonder they looked shell shocked.

"Not all gnomes are bad, not if they do good magic. And you're as good as they come, Lace."

"You promise?"

He put her little hand on his chest. "Cross my heart. Now, let me show you what I wanted you to see."

She nodded, though her lip was still between her teeth.

Brayden touched the coin around his neck, closed his eyes, focusing on the magic within, then opened his palm.

Lacy gasped, and Brayden smiled. He opened his eyes to see the rainbow he'd made parting through the clouds and ending at his palm.

"It's so pretty," Lacy breathed. She held out her hand then stopped.

"It won't hurt. You can hold my hand, and the rainbow will stay." As long as he concentrated, that is.

She worried her lip then pressed her palm against his. Lace let out a giggle as the end of the rainbow wrapped its way around their joined hands like a bow.

"Wow!" Cameron yelled from the doorway then ran to their side, Aiden on his trail.

Brayden looked up to see Allison standing behind them, a look of slight fear in her eyes before she blinked it away.

Damn it. He hadn't meant to show her that he had magic like Greg, though he didn't, not really if what Rina said was true. He'd just have to push harder to show her that magic could be good.

Aiden and Cameron put their hands on top of Lacy's, and the rainbow wrapped around their hands as well.

"Cool," Aiden said under his breath.

"It's beautiful," Lacy said.

Brayden looked at the three of them, smiling, happy as though there wasn't a care in the world, and then he met Allison's gaze.

"Yeah, it's very beautiful," he said, though he wasn't talking to the kids anymore.

Ally stared at him, uncertainty and heat warring in her eyes.

He'd fix this somehow. He'd waited too long for everything to fall through his fingertips.

Brayden wanted the family in front of him, and he'd do anything to make it a reality. He just needed to make sure his luck didn't run out because, for some reason, he knew the danger lurking around their lives was only beginning.

Chapter 6

Allison held her breath as Brayden showed her children the rainbow coming out of his palm. If she hadn't been through so much with the Coopers, she wouldn't have believed it.

Even though the colors were amazingly beautiful, she didn't know if she could trust the effects of magic. After all, she'd been an unknowing victim of magic for twelve years...at least.

She'd also almost lost her children during the Christmas holidays when Jack Frost had attacked Justin and Rina while they were ice-skating with her children.

If she hadn't cared so much for the Coopers, she would have cut herself off from them trying to protect her babies.

But it wouldn't have done any good. No matter how hard she tried to push, magic and the Coopers seemed to surround her life.

Now the man she thought she could see herself with held magic in any way. Even though he'd told her it was good magic, nothing like Greg's, she couldn't be sure. She thought she'd trusted Brayden with everything but her heart, but she could've been wrong.

Her babies were in his hands, and he had the power to make anything come true with luck.

Or at least that's what she thought his magic did. She'd been too stunned when he'd revealed what he was to question what exactly his magic did.

Allison didn't know if she had it in her to be with a man who held that kind of power in his hands. Not that she'd decided to succumb to her own desires. She might want Brayden, not just physically, but in every way irrevocably possible, but that didn't mean she'd give in.

She had more to lose than just her heart, and Brayden was currently holding those things now.

Everything was moving too fast for her and not fast enough. Her arm ached like a bitch, and she just wanted to curl into a ball with some chocolate and wait for everything to get better.

Yeah, like she'd ever done that in her life.

No, she didn't run away from things. She just kept going with the grain, sometimes against it, until she couldn't move anymore. She lived for her kids, not herself. And right now, since she wasn't working and her kids weren't in school because of a man—no, gnome—she was floundering.

And yet, why did she want to set everything aside for a moment and sink into Brayden's arms?

God, she didn't want to be *that* woman. No, she'd rather kick ass than have him fall into her arms. That sounded like a better deal.

Cameron ran up to her and put his arms around her waist. "Why do you look sad, Mom?"

She ruffled his hair and leaned down to inhale that little boy scent. "I'm just worrying, you know me."

"With Brayden and the rest of the Coopers around, nothing can hurt us."

Oh, if only that were true. Though she believed that, with the authorities on David's trail and the Coopers rallying around them, they were safer, that didn't mean they were safe from getting their hearts broken.

"I still want you to think safe, okay? Just because we're staying here with Brayden doesn't mean you can stop looking out for yourself and your brother and sister."

He nodded and rubbed his cast, his eyes looking tired.

"I think it's time you lie down for a bit. What do you say?"

Cam scowled and shook his head. "Aiden and Lacy aren't going to lay down."

"Aiden and Lacy didn't have their arm broken last night."

He let out a putout sigh and rolled his eyes. "Fine."

"Fine is right. You don't have to sleep, just lay down."

He rambled off to his room, or at least the room he was staying in. She didn't want to create those connections and settle down. Not when they'd hopefully be leaving soon.

She couldn't entwine their lives with Brayden's anymore than necessary. It would hurt too much when they had to leave.

"Knock knock," Jordan said as she walked into the house. The alarm immediately sounded, and Jackson came in behind her, turning it off.

"I thought you two would have work today," Brayden said as he walked into the house, Lacy and Aiden by his side.

Bray took off his jacket and brushed a lock of hair from his forehead, and Allison's gaze landed on his chest that filled out his Henley quite nicely.

"I've already done my work for now and can do the rest from home for now," Jordan said as she leaned down to give Aiden a hug.

He blushed and fidgeted in her arms.

Jackson took off his jacket then picked Lacy up for a hug. Allison blinked as Lacy kissed the usually stern man's cheek and hugged him hard. Jackson's cheeks reddened, but he hugged her back.

"I closed down the office today. I figured you guys could use my help."

Everyone froze. Jackson was the only dentist for counties and was frankly a workaholic who *never* took days off.

Miracles of miracles. Scary Jackson Cooper had a heart.

"Thank you, Jacks. And Jordan of course," she said, still surprised they were both here.

Jordan smiled. "Well, we figured you could use a break to go to the sheriff's department to talk to Tyler about last night, plus go to your place and get anything Justin and Rina forgot. Brayden should go with you though so you're not alone."

Allison could have sworn the other woman winked when she said that. Well, it looked as though the Coopers were playing matchmakers as well as protectors. She didn't know quite how she felt about that.

"You're going to babysit?" she asked Jackson, a little worried. It wasn't as if she didn't trust the man, but she wasn't sure she'd ever seen him particularly warm to her children, besides what she'd just seen with Lacy.

Jackson quirked the side of his mouth up in a semblance of a smile. "I did help raise my four younger brothers, in case you've forgotten."

Allison blushed, ashamed. "I'm sorry; I don't mean to be rude."

Brayden came up behind her and wrapped an arm around her waist. She stiffened at the obvious show of affection in front of his family. What on earth could that man be thinking?

"You're not rude. Jacks just doesn't show off his Babysitter's Club side often."

Jackson shook his head and, with Lacy still in his arms, turned toward the living room. "I'm going to let Lacy show me what toys she brought with her. You two go do what you need to. We'll hold down the fort."

He walked away with Lacy in his arms, Aiden trailing behind him.

"Okay, who was that man?" Jordan asked.

Brayden laughed. "Jacks isn't that bad, you know."

"Oh, I do," Allison said. "But, this doesn't seem like him."

"Tell me about it. When he offered to come with me today, Matt nearly passed out."

They laughed, and Allison couldn't help noticing Brayden's arm was still around her, even though she didn't need the support...well, at least physically. His warmth felt damn good on her, not that she'd say that out loud.

"Okay, you two go off and talk to Tyler. We'll be here if you need us."

Jordan followed Jackson and the kids and left Allison standing in the foyer alone with Brayden. Allison held up her hand and ran behind them, making sure she said goodbye to her children before she left.

"With Jordan here with her magic, that you know and trust, the kids should be safe," Brayden said as he bundled her up, his fingers dancing along her neck as he helped with her jacket.

Shivers ran down her spine that had nothing to do with the cold. Allison ignored them, and they piled in his truck, her hands shaking.

"I know she'll take care of them. I'm just worried like a normal mom. I have a list though of what we need so that shouldn't take long. I'm just not in the mood to have to relive everything that happened last night when we talk with Tyler."

Brayden pulled out of the garage and held her hand. "I won't let you be alone."

She warmed at his words but shook them off.

"Don't do that," she said.

"What?"

"Don't treat me like this. Bray. I know I kissed you back today, but I shouldn't have. We can't be together. Don't you get that? I need to make sure my children are safe. I don't have time to worry about myself. I can't be selfish. And yes, I know in my heart that you're not Greg. I trust you Brayden, even with the magic thing that I just don't know about. But it's change. You know? I can't deal with all of this and take care of my children."

He squeezed her hand but didn't say anything for a while as they drove toward the station.

God, she'd ruined it. She'd only meant to protect herself and her children, and she'd hurt Brayden...and herself, in the process. She didn't deserve him.

"Don't count me out yet, Ally. I won't stand in your way of being the best mom you can be, but at some point, you need to realize it's all right to be a woman too."

"I can't, Bray."

"No, you can, but you aren't. You won't. That's the difference. You're scared, and I know you have a right to be. But I want you to take a chance. I've been standing on the sidelines for ten years because I thought that was what I had to do and I was wrong. I'm not going to let you through my fingers again. I'm not losing you. I came to close to it before and I'm not letting that happen."

"Bray..."

"No, don't say anything. Let's talk to Tyler and get it over with. Then we can talk about us."

"There is no us."

"There will be."

"Brayden..."

"I'm lucky, remember? It's time I use my lucky talisman for something other than myself."

They got out of the car and headed into the station. The cop on duty in the front of house let them go straight back to Tyler's office, though Allison could feel the stares of the people in the room as Brayden put his hand on the small of her back.

She could only imagine the rumor mill at this point, considering she and her children were living with the man.

Tyler opened his arms, and she went in for a quick hug when she walked into his office. She'd always hugged the Coopers like they were her family and hadn't thought anything of it until she heard that growl come from Brayden again. It'd never been a problem. But of course, that was before she'd found out that his feelings went beyond a cup of coffee and she'd felt his lips against hers.

Something he wanted to do again.

Something she desperately wanted to do again but knew she shouldn't.

Tyler raised a brow but didn't say anything, sitting down in his chair behind his big desk.

"Let's make this quick because I can't really say everything, right?" Tyler asked, and Allison nodded.

Brayden took her hand in his, and she held on for dear life. She didn't care if it made her look weak; she needed his strength.

She was tired of being strong for herself when she had no one to lean on. Maybe she could just relax for a little while. But that didn't seem fair to Brayden or her.

She told Tyler what had happened that night and earlier that day in the diner. Though she knew he already knew most of it through Rina and talking to her in the hospital. But apparently droning on about every detail was a part of police work. She knew they wouldn't put the magic elements in the report, but the fact that Greg's family wanted her kids was something that couldn't be ignored. Yes, she was afraid of their magic, but that didn't mean they could tell the world.

Greg's family didn't have a leg to stand on concerning custody, but that didn't matter to gnomes apparently. Well, it didn't matter to regular people either. The fact that they seemed like they were going to go after them no matter what, meant legal procedures meant nothing.

"We'll do all we can. I know you need to get back to work and your kids need to get to school, so we'll be sure we have someone watching you guys as much as possible," Tyler said as they finished up.

"But what about everything else in town? You can't drop everything just for us."

"We can, and we will. But honestly, all of us Coopers can help too. It's not just a law enforcement problem, Ally."

Yes, the gnomes were something involving magic. Something that she didn't understand.

Allison looked over at Brayden and thought about the magic around his neck and shuddered. Everything seemed out of her control, and she hated it. It made no sense not to like his magic because of Greg. Maybe it was because everything was moving so fast.

They said their goodbyes, and Brayden drove them to her apartment. Seeing the shabby place after spending the night at

Brayden's made her feel insignificant, as though she couldn't care for her children.

With a brave smile pasted on her face, she walked up the steps to her place, Brayden on her heels. She could only imagine what he thought of her apartment. Still, it was hers, something she could afford, and it had kept her babies safe.

At least it had until now.

There was a new door in place, and she froze. She didn't have the keys to this door. How was she going to get in?

"Crap, I forgot, sorry." Brayden dug into his pocket, and Allison tried not to stare at how well he filled out his jeans. "Jordan gave me a key. Matt fixed your door this morning. I'm sorry."

She shook her head. "It's fine. That was nice of Matt. How much do I owe him?"

"Nothing."

"Bray." She would not be in debt to another Cooper.

"No really. He charged the apartment complex. If they charge you extra on your rent, let us know because it's the facility's problem, not yours."

She nodded, feeling silly that she'd been so defensive over money.

Brayden followed behind her and closed the door.

"Damn, the power's out," Brayden said.

"I have some candles that we can light."

Oh, great, Brayden Cooper by candlelight. That can't end well. Or it will end too well.

"I'll just start packing. You can hang out I guess." She turned and saw Brayden staring at the floor. She looked down and froze.

The bloodstain had been smaller when she remembered it. God, that was a little too close to everything going from bad to worse for her.

Brayden pulled her into a tight hug, his nose against her neck, and she felt him inhale. She wrapped her arms around his waist, letting her hands roam up his back.

She'd been so scared, but as soon as Brayden had walked through the door, she'd felt better.

"I almost lost you," he said, his rumbling voice low, deep, sliding over her body like silk.

"But I'm fine," she said soothingly and let her hands slide under his shirt, gasping at the heat radiating from him like a furnace.

He pulled back and ran his hands up her sides slowly. "I don't know what I'd do if I lost you. I just found you."

"Bray..."

"I know I don't have you. Not yet. But I'm not giving up without a fight. I've loved you for ten years, Allison. I'm not going away anytime soon."

She pulled back slightly, stunned. "Ten...ten years?"

He nodded, his jaw firm. "I've sat back and watched you in a relationship you hated.

Then I stood back and tried to be the friend you could count on, all the while holding back my feelings. I don't want to do that anymore, Ally. I want to be with you."

"How could you love me? We're not even together." Though when she said the words, she knew exactly how, considering she loved him too.

"Just because I couldn't be with you doesn't mean I don't know you, Allison."

"I care about you," she started, knowing she hadn't said the words she felt, the words he needed to hear. She saw the flash of hurt in his eyes but didn't stop. "I can't make any promises. I stayed with a man I didn't love because of magic. I don't know if I can trust anything having to do with it, Bray."

"I would never use magic on you."

"I know, and I trust you. That scares me because I don't know why I do. I want you, Bray. I know I shouldn't. I know I should walk away right now and take my kids and find a way to live without you. But I don't want to. Not now."

"Then let's live right here. Right now."

"I don't get to decide my own fate. I have to put my kids first."

"I'm not saying we should ignore them. I love those kids, Ally."

"I know you do. That's why I'm in this room with you in the first place. If you didn't care for my kids, I wouldn't be here. I just don't know, Bray. Everything is just moving too fast right now, and I have to think."

"Don't think. I'm going to kiss you, Ally. And then maybe do something more. And when it's over, and you're gasping for air, then we can talk about the future and everything that it brings. But for just once in your life, live for the moment. Live for yourself."

Her body warmed at his words, and she let him tip her face up so he could capture her lips in a bruising, yet, sweet kiss.

Allison parted her lips, letting his tongue dance with hers. She ran her hands up higher on his back, scoring her nails down when she exhaled.

"Fuck," he breathed. "You taste like sin and happiness, Ally."

She let out a laugh. "I like that."

He grinned, his eyes full of intent. "Good, then you'll really like this."

He ran his hands down her sides, brushing against her skin as he trailed his fingers up her shirt along her spine. Tendrils of pleasure wound their way through her, leaving heat along the wake.

Brayden kissed her again, this time harder, with a purpose.

She couldn't believe she was doing this. There was a madman out there waiting to take her babies, and she was kissing...and probably doing more...with a man she knew more than anyone yet hadn't even held a real conversation with about who they were.

God, she couldn't do this.

Brayden pulled back and framed her face. "Stop thinking so much, Ally."

She looked into his deep blue eyes and shook her head. "We can't do this, Bray. I'm no good for you. All I bring is trouble, and I don't even know if we'd have a future. You deserve something better. You deserve a real family to fill up that home of yours where you can create your own memories, not just take all the trouble that comes with mine."

Brayden tucked a lock of hair behind her ear. "You're wrong. You're beyond wrong. I don't know what our future is, Ally, but I know I don't want mine to be with anyone else. I've had years, *years*, to find someone, and I couldn't. You know why? Because I'd already found her but I couldn't have her. I'm not going to let someone hurt you or your babies, and I'm not going to stand by and watch you walk away."

"Brayden, we're not a couple. Not really. I can't just jump into a relationship. Not after..."

She couldn't say that last part. Even though it had been magic keeping her there— something else standing in the way of her and Bray—she couldn't forget what Greg had done.

She could never forget.

"Ally, what happened with Greg? I think I know, but I'm hoping my imagination is far worse than anything that could have happened."

He wrapped his arms around her waist, anchoring her to him for more than just that moment.

Allison let out a shaky breath, her knees growing weak, though Brayden held her up. He was always holding her up lately. God, she hated it. She wanted, no *needed*, to hold herself up.

She couldn't rely on any man.

She pulled back slightly, putting distance between them. She caught the flash of hurt on his face before he covered it up.

Damn it, she wasn't good at this.

She didn't deserve him or his love.

"Ally."

"Greg was what you think and worse," she let out. "He forced me to stay with him even when I tried to go. I know men do that without magic and I thought that was all it was. Even that makes me sick, but now I find out it's magic? For so long I thought I'd just been weak. One of those woman who made excuses for him even though I hadn't known it."

Brayden shook his head and pulled her close. She didn't fight him, needing his warmth even if she hated herself for it.

"He used magic, Ally. It wasn't your fault."

"I know that now, but I didn't for so long. He had to have everything his way, and it had to be perfect. And if it wasn't..."

Brayden touched her cheek, but she didn't flinch. God, she trusted this man, despite the magic that ran through his veins.

"And if it wasn't?" Brayden prompted.

"He made sure his displeasure was known." She lifted her chin, daring Brayden to say anything about that.

His jaw clenched, and he growled that growl she was just getting used to hearing. "I'd go back and kill him myself if I could."

"Well, the car accident that killed him made it too easy," she said. "He died on impact. But I'd help you kill him if I could, not only for hurting me physically, emotionally, and everywhere in between, but for what he did to my kids."

Brayden's grip tightened for a moment before he visibly forced himself to relax. "Did he touch them, Ally?"

She shook her head. "No, he never hit them. Though I don't know what would have happened if he'd lived." She swallowed the bile that had risen at that thought. But Greg was gone now and couldn't hurt her children. Though his brother endangered them, she wouldn't let that stop her kids from living a normal life.

Well, as normal as they could, being half gnome living in a paranormal town.

"What did he do?"

"He hit me, yelled at me, criticized me. The normal stuff." She tried to sound flippant, but she knew Brayden could see right through her.

"Nothing is normal about this, Ally. What he did to you isn't *normal*. I want you to see that being with a man doesn't mean pain, but respect and love. That's my goal in all this."

"Bray..."

"What else did he do? Because I know there's something more. Something that haunts Aiden."

Tears filled her eyes, and she swallowed. She could never hide anything from Brayden, even when she so desperately wanted to forget.

"Greg got mad one night, madder than usual. Aiden had left something on the table; I don't even remember what. He went after him, but I stood in the way. There was no way he was going to hurt my son. That only enraged Greg more, and he knocked me to the ground, kicking me in the stomach as hard as he could."

Brayden stroked her back, calming her even though her emotions ran ragged.

"I was pregnant at the time, though I hadn't known it."

Brayden sucked in a sharp breath then crushed her to his body. Tears tore from her, long wrenching sobs that made her shake.

God, it hurt so much. She'd lost so much.

"I'm so sorry, Ally."

"I took myself to the doctor, but Greg caught up with me. I don't remember what happened from there, only that everyone forgot what had happened. But not me, not Aiden."

"Damn his magic," Brayden whispered, his breath warm on her ear as she hugged him tight. "But it's not my magic. Do you understand that?"

"I want to."

"Then we'll make it happen."

"Bray, I don't know if I can have kids now. I have the three most beautiful children already...but since...I just don't know."

He kissed her then. A soft, slow, emotion-filled kiss that took her breath away. His lips lingered at the corner of her mouth, searching, needing. She leaned in, letting his tongue brush hers, the taste of coffee intertwined with that just-Bray taste.

"Then we'll figure it out."

"Bray..."

"No, just let me love you. Not here, not now. But let me show you what I mean by my actions, not just my words. Let yourself lean on me, and I'll do the same to you. That way it's not one sided."

"How did you know that's what I was scared of?" How did he know her so well?

"Because I know you, Allison Malone. I'm not giving up. I was quiet for way too long, and I'm making up for lost time."

"I don't know, Bray."

"Then we'll go slow."

Allison leaned into his hold, and they stood in the living room, wrapped in each other, knowing the world beckoned and sweet words weren't the way to get things done.

She knew she could trust him; that wasn't the problem. It was trusting herself when she was with him that caused doubt. She just didn't know if she was worth enough to make it work.

In his arms, though, it didn't matter, at least for the moment. But moments end, and life would come calling...just not right now.

Chapter 7

Aiden couldn't believe his mom and Brayden had actually let them go to school. He'd thought his mom would lock him in a padded room or wrapped him in bubble wrap before she'd let it happen.

She was a little overprotective like that.

Well, considering his uncle, or whatever that man was, wanted him and his brother and sister, he guessed he didn't blame his mom all that much.

But, really, a boy—almost a man at this point really—needed some space.

But, she'd talked with the Coopers, and now he was at school with his brother and sister. His mom had told him to watch out for his brother and sister because, even though they hadn't heard from his dad's brother in a couple days, that didn't mean the danger was gone.

Great, just what he needed. To watch over Cameron and Lacy even though they weren't even in the same grade. He wished he lived in a bigger town where there was a middle school, but no, he was forced to stay in the same school as his baby brother and sister until next year.

Well, it wasn't all that bad. Now he was in the oldest class on campus, so he ruled. At least in his mind anyway. Most kids didn't like hanging out with the Malones since they considered them trash.

Well, screw them.

He looked over his shoulder on the playground, sure his mom was around the corner listening to his thoughts—she was creepy like that sometimes—but he didn't think she would be around. Not with Brayden in her life now.

He didn't know what he thought about that. His mom was an adult, and he guessed that she needed a boyfriend or whatever, but it still felt weird.

He'd never really liked his dad, even though he didn't think kids were supposed to think that. But, his dad wasn't a nice guy, and he'd made their mom cry.

A lot.

Brayden made her smile, and Aiden really liked the guy. Even though Brayden wasn't his dad, he was way better. He actually listened when Aiden or his brother and sister talked. He took him to play baseball when his mom had to work.

Aiden guessed if Brayden made his mom happy, then he was a pretty good guy.

That didn't mean Aiden was completely happy about it though. What if Brayden didn't want kids that weren't his own? Yeah, the guy liked hanging out with them now, but what if Brayden and his mom got married?

He'd have to talk with him, even though he didn't really want to. But ever since his dad had died, he was the man of the house now, so he had to take the responsibility.

He had to take care of Cameron and Lacy. Even now he watched them play on the playground. Cameron was showing his friends his new cast and having them sign it with the felt tip maker he brought with him while Lacy was playing in the field watching fairies or some crap. His little sister was way too girly for him.

Aiden knew he wasn't the only one watching them either. Justin, Abby, and other Coopers were around making sure everyone was safe. That was good at least. He didn't want to lose his brother and sister, even if they annoyed him sometimes.

A strange tingling ran over his skin, and he shuddered. Something like little pinpricks, like when Lacy rolled Cameron's cars over his arms, but harder, slid over him. What was that? He looked around but didn't see anything, just kids playing, not noticing whatever had made him feel weird.

He looked over at Cameron and met his brother's eyes. There was fear in them. He didn't like seeing his little brother scared and it made him even more scared. What was going on?

So, Cameron had felt it too?

Aiden stiffened and looked over to where Lacy had been playing, and ice settled in his chest.

Where was she?

Gone. No, that didn't make any sense. She'd just been there playing. He looked around and thought he saw a glimmer of her pigtails far away from where she had been. He turned toward the adults, but they didn't look as if anything was wrong. In fact, they kind of had a glassy look in their eyes, as if they had gone blind or drunk or something.

Magic?

What if his uncle used gnome magic? Hadn't his mom said that gnomes could make people do or see things? Then why did Cameron and he not see what the gnomes wanted?

Maybe it was because they were gnomes too, or at least half gnomes.

Fear shook at him, and he nodded to Cameron to tell the adults. Well, at least that's what he hoped. He needed to get to his sister and he hoped his little brother would know what to do.

He had to find Lacy. If he was the only one other than his little brother who could sense something was wrong, maybe he was the only one who could find her.

His mom had told him to watch her, and he'd failed. He didn't want his little sister to be hurt.

Aiden zipped his coat tighter against the wind and followed the path where Lacy had been, climbing through a hole in the fence that he was pretty sure hadn't been there before.

The bad man wouldn't hurt his little sister. Not on his watch.

****

Brayden walked through the doors of the school after he'd had his coffee with Allison at the diner. He'd left her alone after she'd begged him, even though he'd rather have been by her side. She'd argued that they all needed to work and try to live their lives while focusing on keeping her children safe.

He could understand that, but he still wanted to lock her and the kids up in his house and pamper them until everything was safe.

Tyler had done a background check on David Malone's family and had come up with nothing out of the ordinary. Apparently Greg and David's parents lived five hours away in a small home while David lived down the street. The father, Gerald, had been questioned in several suspicious deaths though he had always had an alibi and witnesses aren't reliable. No charges would stick. With the magic they possessed, though, people might not have even noticed something was off around them.

A scary as fuck feeling.

Yet the emotions running through him were even scarier, even though he was pretty sure he could face those in a heartbeat. He wanted Allison in his home, his bed, and everywhere in between. She'd already settled in his heart far easier than he'd have thought. Well, she'd always been there, but now it felt as if there was a future.

When she'd finally broken and explained what her bastard of a husband had done to her, he'd fought the urge to find Greg's grave, unbury him, and beat the shit out of his bones.

Morbid, but worth it.

Brayden had known Allison was strong as hell, but he hadn't known how strong. The fact that she'd lost a child...

He took a deep breath, trying to calm down. He knew he'd never be able to give back what had been so ruthlessly taken from her, but he'd find a way to keep her smiling. Keep her babies smiling.

It was the least he could do.

He probably should have been at work, but he didn't care. He had enough money, and the people who worked for him could handle things for a while. He'd trained his staff so they were the best out there and didn't need him anymore beyond paperwork and his own desire to work with his hands. His family came first.

His family.

Brayden smiled at that. Oh yes, he'd make sure Allison, Aiden, Cameron, and Lacy were his family. There was no way he'd let them become less significant in his life.

He just needed to convince Allison of that.

He picked up his visitor badge from the front office and walked to the back because he knew it was recess time. Justin had told him he'd watch the Malone kids, but Brayden wanted to be there.

The hair on the back of neck stood on end...

Something was wrong.

He pushed open the back door as Cameron changed directions and ran toward him, tears running down his cheeks, his cast flailing as he waved Brayden down.

Brayden stood on alert, catching Cameron as he ran into his arms, but checking his surroundings. He didn't see anyone else yelling or running from the playground...but he couldn't see Aiden or Lacy.

"What is it, Cam?" he asked as he knelt down to be at the boy's eye level.

"Nobody felt it, but we did," he said through sobs.

Brayden shook his head then wiped Cameron's cheeks. "Take a deep breath and slow down, buddy. I don't understand what you're saying. Where are Lacy and Aiden?"

His heart beat against his chest in a staccato that threatened to steal his breath.

"What didn't anyone else feel, Cam?" he asked when Cameron took deep, gasping breaths.

"It was like something blocking out the noise, you know? No one else noticed it, but I think Aiden did. Then we looked to where Lacy was playing in the yard, and she wasn't there anymore. Aiden went after her, and I came to you. Well, I was going to go to the other people, but then I saw you."

Fear clawed at his belly as he heard Cameron's words and the meaning beneath them.

"Bray!" Justin yelled as he ran to his side. "I can't find Lacy and Aiden. It's weird. One minute they're there, the next, they're gone. I don't know what the hell happened. I was inside for just a minute and I felt like something washed over me, and it made everyone stop what they were doing. I ran outside as soon as I could, but it was too late." His brother's face was pale, his voice shaky.

Fuck, they'd failed. They'd all failed. Brayden should have been there.

"Cam said that, too. Lacy was there one minute, the next she wasn't. Aiden went after her."

Justin cursed under his breath. "Why the hell did I have to go inside at the minute? I would have been outside and been able to help if I hadn't had to deal with that sick kid."

Brayden looked around, noticing they were drawing a crowd, kids and adults alike. "Get the kids back in their classrooms. I'm taking Cam with me to get Ally and call Tyler. We'll find them. It wasn't your fault." *No, it was mine.* "They have magic, remember?" He whispered that last part, knowing there were straining ears around them.

Justin nodded, though Brayden could tell from the look on his brother's face that Justin still blamed himself. Brayden took Cameron's hand and walked him out to his truck. He called Tyler first, wanting to make sure Ty kept a lookout, then dialed the diner.

"Bray? What's wrong?" The fear in Allison's voice made him want to punch something.

"I think they took Lacy, Ally," he said, wanting to get the words out quickly before he broke down right along with Cameron. "Aiden followed them, but I have Cam with me. I'm calling Rina so she can come get you. We'll find them, Ally."

He heard her trying to control her breathing for a full minute before she said anything. "I'll be ready," she said, her voice firm, yet hollow.

God, she was the strongest woman he'd ever known.

His hands shaking, he called Rina, while Cameron stayed silent by his side, the tears no longer coming, but his body seemingly broken beyond just a fractured arm.

Rina picked up and he explained what happened and she cursed and said she was coming after she picked up Allison. "Bray, if David used magic on the adults, he could maybe use it on you. I'm not sure since you Coopers are in a league of your own. But, what I think is happening is David is using all he can to get those kids. When the magic and glamour wears off, there's going to be hell to pay for David because we're going to kick his ass, but the adults won't remember a thing. That might be a good thing considering we don't want them to know about all the magic."

Brayden held Cameron to his side for the few minutes they waited for Allison to come. Rina pulled up, screeching tires as she parked.

"Cam?" Allison wrenched open the door and held her son to her chest. Cameron didn't cry but held on for dear life.

"What happened?" she asked as she leaned into Brayden's hold.

"We're not sure," Brayden said, pissed at himself for not knowing more. "I think David used magic and distracted the rest of the yard, taking Lacy from recess. Cam said that Aiden followed her, which scares the hell out of me."

Allison nodded, rubbing small circles on Cameron's arm. Her gaze caught Brayden's for a moment, her eyes filled with so much fear and sorrow that Brayden brought them both into his arms hard and never wanted to let go.

But, there wasn't time for that. No, he needed to find the other two kids that felt like his own.

Rina ran toward them from where she'd been talking to Tyler. "Tyler's out looking in the woods behind the school," Rina explained.

"Everyone else is out looking as well. I mean, the Coopers anyway. Tyler can't call a town-wide search because of the magic involved. It'd be too dangerous." Her mouth thinned, and she shook her head.

"Rina? Can you watch Cam while Bray and I look for my children?" Allison asked, her voice filled with far more control than he thought she'd have at this point.

Rina nodded and tried to smile at Cameron, though everyone saw through it. Cameron just stood there blankly. "Sure. I can do that. I'll go to Bray's; how's that? Just in case the kids go back there."

Brayden gave her his house key, relieved that someone was thinking past going full out and looking for Lacy and Aiden.

He knelt down at Cameron's level and took him by the shoulders. "We're going to find your brother and sister, you got me?"

Cameron nodded. "Take care of mom, okay?"

Brayden crooked his mouth in what he hoped was a reassuring smile. "Always, Cam, always."

After Allison said her goodbyes, he took her by the hand, and they walked behind the school, aware they weren't hiding everything from the town. But, at this point, he didn't care. He just wanted to find his children.

He tripped over a rock then squeezed Allison's hand.

His children.

Fuck, he hadn't even had Allison in his life as more than a friend for more than a few moments, and he already thought of them as his. But, the fear running through his veins was a father's fear. The love he felt when he joked with Cameron, listened to Aiden, or felt Lacy's little hand in his was a father's love.

He wasn't going to lose those kids.

"I'm sorry, Ally."

"It wasn't your fault. But when I find David, I'm going to cut off his balls. That bastard can't hurt my babies and get away with it."

He smiled despite himself. "If we weren't in the situation we're in, I'd say that was fucking hot despite being scary as hell."

She tried to smile but failed. "Help me find my babies and we'll talk, okay?"

"We will, Ally. Aiden wasn't taken as far as we know. Hopefully, the kid will be smart and leave a trail."

Allison nodded, her shoulders straightening. "He's a smart boy, but why the hell did he leave like that?"

"Because his sister was in trouble and there was no one else around to help her. He's like you, you know. Putting himself at risk to save Lacy. You're raising him well."

When they reached Tyler, she stopped and kissed Brayden's cheek. "Thanks for that," she whispered.

"Ally, where's Cam?" Tyler asked, his gaze sharpened.

"With Rina."

"You should be with him. We'll find your kids, Ally."

"I don't think so. I'm staying by Bray's side, and we're going to find my babies. Now tell me what you've found out so far."

Damn, he liked this fierce side of her.

Tyler looked taken aback for a moment before lowering his brows. "Fine. We're going to fan out and keep looking. We've found a trail that we think Aiden made out through the forest, but then we lost it. By the way, the *we* in that is the Coopers. I can't get my department involved because of the magic. I'm going to have to find a way around that in the future because this shit keeps happening. There needs to be law enforcement of some kind to deal with the magic."

"I don't really care about that right now, Ty. Just tell me where Bray and I need to go. We're losing time."

Brayden squeezed her hand, letting her handle talking to Ty since she seemed to need the control.

"I want you guys to head east along the trail we've marked. We're fanning out because David is hiding his tracks well enough that he could be anywhere. Stay together and use these." He handed them each hand-held radios. "Cell reception sucks once you get in the deep brush. Stay warm and let us know what's up. We'll find them, Ally."

She nodded, and Brayden took her toward where the trail started.

"I'm not going to let anything happen to you," Brayden promised as they walked through the woods, the sun slowly fading away through the thick branches.

"I don't care what happens to me. I just want my children to be okay."

"Well, I care what happens to you. And so does Cam and half a dozen other people, so let's just be safe, okay?"

"I'm glad you're here with me."

"There's nowhere else I'd rather be. I love you." He knew he was bearing his soul to her, but she already owned it.

She let out a sigh as they both looked for any sign of her son. "I love you too, you big dolt, but this isn't the time or place for that. Let's find my children."

Brayden swallowed hard at her words. Damn, she loved him. Thank God it wasn't only one sided. But, now wasn't the time to think about that. They'd deal with what all that meant when they were safe.

Maybe his luck wouldn't just run to numbers and a job; maybe it would be something more. But after this, after the fact that he couldn't find the children he called his own, he felt like his luck was changing. Everything was falling apart around him. Even though Allison had said she loved him, they were still in a state of stasis until David could be caught.

Luck didn't come from an inevitable, but from chance.

Maybe his lucky coin wasn't so lucky after all.

They searched for another few hours, desperation settling in as they searched blindly once they moved beyond the obvious trail. The wind slid through the gaps in the trees, cooling their skin with each passing minute, the icy tendrils of lost hope seeping into their bones.

Just because the trail had started in the woods didn't mean it would end there. From the conversations on the radio, he knew Matt and Jordan were searching around town while Jackson searched on the west end of the woods. Justin and Abby couldn't leave the school, and Rina was at Brayden's home with Cameron.

"We have to find them," Allison whispered.

Brayden stopped and brought her into his arms. She sank into his hold easily, as though they'd been holding each other for years rather than dancing round it for that much longer.

"We will, but we'll have to head back soon. I need to make sure you're safe and healthy. And don't start, I know you can go on for hours, but you can't wear yourself down to the bone."

She shook her head and glared at him. "I'm not quitting."

He framed her face and stole a kiss from her soft lips. "Never. But we need to get water, flashlights, and other provisions for later. Right now, we just have ourselves for an initial search. I also think Tyler needs to get the rest of the force involved. We don't have to mention the magic if we can help it, but it's time."

She shuddered in his hold. "I know. I just don't want to leave. What if we miss something?"

"I know how you feel. We'll search for another thirty minutes and head back for supplies. Okay?"

She nodded, and he took her hand while they headed farther into the woods, praying for any sign of Lacy and Aiden. He cursed himself when he thought of how ill prepared they were. He didn't even have a fucking weapon if he came upon David, though he knew Tyler would want them to wait for him to deal with the security of the situation anyway.

"Mom?"

Brayden and Allison turned to the right at the sound of Aiden's voice, Brayden's heart practically beating out of his chest.

"Oh, God, Aiden." Allison jumped over a fallen tree and pulled Aiden into her arms.

Brayden was right behind her, pulling them both to his chest even as he surveyed the area for anything else out of place. He couldn't be too careful, not with the fragile cargo in his hold.

"I'm sorry I left, Mom. But I couldn't just let Lacy go like that."

Chills ran down his spine. "It's okay, Aiden. You're safe now."

Allison's tears finally fell, and she held Aiden closer.

"I found Lacy, Bray," Aiden said, his voice muffled through Allison's arms.

Allison pulled back, and Brayden ran a hand down her hair. "Where, Aiden?"

"He's in a cave on the other side of a group of fallen trees. I know where he is and can take you there."

Allison shook her head. "No, I don't want you anywhere near him."

Aiden raised his chin. "But I know where they are, and you can't just leave me here."

Brayden met Allison's gaze. Aiden was right. They couldn't leave him in the middle of the forest alone, and he was the only one who knew where Lacy was. He had to go with them, though that didn't mean they had to like it.

"Fine, but you stay here and let me and Brayden take care of it."

"Actually, Ally, if there's a fight, you need to let me take care of it and get your kids to safety."

"Bray."

"It's not a man-woman thing. It's a training thing. I can fight; you can't. Tyler made sure all of us at least knew some form of skill to protect ourselves. Plus, I want you to get Lacy and Aiden out. They're the more important things here."

"I don't want to lose you either," she said, her voice fierce.

"You won't. If something happens, you take the kids and call Tyler later after I radio in. We should tell him anyway, so he can head here."

He gave their relative position to Tyler as best he could, and his brother told them to stay put.

Right. That wasn't going to happen.

Yeah, it'd be stupid, but they weren't just going to stand there, not when Lacy was so close.

They turned down the sound on the radio so they could sneak up on David and followed Aiden's direction around a grouping of trees. Though it was hard to find, he could see the dark cave opening where Aiden said David held Lacy.

Brayden held back the revulsion at the thought of that man with his little girl—yes, *his* little girl—and held Allison's hand. Even though the Malones seemed to want to only bring them in the family fold, it didn't stop the thoughts entering his mind.

"Stay here," Brayden ordered. He kissed Allison hard on the mouth, aware Aiden was watching them.

When he pulled back, her eyes were wide.

"I'm going with you," she countered, not commenting on the kiss he'd laid on her in front of her son.

"It's not safe."

"Then you shouldn't be alone. Aiden and I won't go in with you, but we'll stay close. We're not letting you go alone, Brayden."

"Yeah, I'm stronger than I look," Aiden argued.

Brayden sighed. "I know, Aid. But I don't want you to get hurt."

"Well, we don't want you to get hurt either. We're coming," Aiden said, and Allison nodded in agreement.

"Fine, but if I tell you to run, you run. Got it?"

"Okay," Allison said, and he believed her. She wouldn't put Aiden at risk.

They made their way to the edge of the cave, the trees providing cover. He peeked around the corner and saw Lacy tied up with rope, her mouth covered with duct tape, but otherwise she looked unharmed.

Thank God.

Still, he'd kill the fucker for touching one hair on her head.

He looked beyond Lacy and didn't see David, but that didn't mean he wasn't there. Brayden picked up a large stick—the only weapon he could find—and slowly crept into the cave. Lacy saw him, and her eyes widened, but he put a finger over his mouth to indicate she shouldn't make a sound even through the duct tape.

David was nowhere to be found, something that scared the hell out of him. Lacy didn't move, but her body shook. He couldn't sense anything around him that could indicate David was around and he didn't understand it. He made his way to Lacy's side, and as he touched her arm, something smashed against his shoulder.

Pain ricocheted down his arm, and he fell to his knees. He heard Lacy's muffled screaming behind the tape, and he turned around to see David hurl a large rock toward them. He lurched out of the way and pulled Lacy with him, covering her with his body.

He didn't have time to undo the knots or uncover her mouth, but he could at least make sure David didn't harm her.

Brayden twisted and stood as David came at him. He used his stick to knock another rock out of David's hands and punched the fucker in the face.

"Don't' get up." Brayden said as he kicked David in the side and moved back to get Lacy. She was more important than hurting the man who had hurt her.

"I'm a gnome. One of the last of my kind. Those kids you so desire are half my blood. My parents are going to raise them with the values and magic they deserve. They're not going to be raised by some whiney-ass human."

Seriously? All of this because of the gnome blood in their veins? Yes, Brayden had known that, but he'd had thought that maybe the Malones would have another reason. But it didn't matter, David was still a kidnapper.

Lacy cried behind him, and he picked her up, ropes and all.

"Ally!" he called. "Come get Lace while I deal with David."

"Lacy!" she yelled back.

David came at him again but stopped, and Brayden felt magic wash over him. Hell, it looked like Rina was right and the Coopers seemed to be immune to gnome magic— something they'd have to deal with later.

"It doesn't work, David," he countered and punched the man in the gut.

He left David writhing on the floor behind him. The man was just a weakling, nothing in the scheme of things. He'd only gotten away with what he had because of the magic he possessed, not through any form of strength or wits. Brayden would just leave him for Tyler. The bastard wasn't worth Brayden's time. All he wanted was to take care of his family.

"You bastard!" David yelled behind him, and Brayden turned to the side at the mouth of the cave, protecting Lacy with his body.

David ran past them and tripped, stumbling across the rock face and tumbling down the hill. Brayden sat Lacy on a rock and undid her tape, then covered her eyes and ears as David fell over the side of the small cliff, screaming in agony until finally David's cries stopped altogether.

Dear God. The man had fallen by tripping.

Tripping.

Apparently he was in shock if he could be so flip at the moment.

"Lacy!" Allison yelled as she ran toward them.

"Be careful, don't trip." Brayden warned and shifted his eyes so he could show her where David had fallen.

"What was that terrible scream?"

Brayden shook his head and Allison's eyes widened, and she pulled Aiden closer. Brayden undid Lacy's ropes then Allison pulled her into her arms.

"Oh, my baby. Did he hurt you?"

"No," Lacy choked out, tears running down her face. "He just tied me up and said he wanted me to go with Grandma and Grandpa. I don't want to go with them."

Brayden pulled Aiden into his side and ran a hand down Lacy's back. "You won't have to. Ever."

Allison nodded. "You're staying with us, baby. You'll never have to go with them."

Brayden looked into her eyes and wanted to know exactly who *us* was, but that would be for another time. Even though David wasn't a problem anymore, he knew the grandparents wouldn't stop. Their fight for the kids probably wasn't over. Not by a long shot.

"Brayden!" Tyler called as he appeared over the rise, the rest of his brothers behind him. "What happened?"

"David tripped," Brayden said honestly as he dipped his hand toward and down the cliff.

Tyler's eyes widened, walked over to the edge and looked down. "Well, shit."

"Mommy, Tyler said shit," Lacy whispered, and Brayden held back a laugh.

Things weren't back to normal, not even close, but once they had Cameron in their hold, they could at least move one step closer to a relationship. Just because the immediate danger was gone, though, didn't mean he'd let them out of his life. No, we wanted them forever.

He just needed to convince Allison of that.

And, by the look on her son's face, Aiden needed a bit of convincing as well.

Chapter 8

Allison ran a hand down Lacy's hair as her baby slept. She was surprised her daughter could sleep now considering Allison wasn't sure she, herself would ever be able to sleep again. Whenever she closed her eyes, she thought of the look on her baby's face with the rope tied around her little wrists.

That wasn't something a mother could forget.

That wasn't something a mother should have to live through.

Allison stood up and tiptoed out of the room, tears threatening to choke her. She didn't want to cry in front of Lacy and wake her up. Her little girl needed as much sleep as possible.

Blindly, she walked down the hallway and ran into a solid chest, startling her.

Brayden.

Wordlessly, he wrapped his arms around her, and she shuddered in his hold, finally letting go of the emotions she had ignored during the ordeal. She'd been so scared they wouldn't make it in time.

A mother shouldn't have to deal with the threat of losing her children like that.

Like anything.

When they'd run through the forest looking for Aiden and then Lacy, she'd tried to remain strong, but it had only been a facade. Inside, she'd wanted to cry, scream, and run. Every step that took her further from what she'd known and closer to the unknown perils of almost losing her children had broken her.

She'd never thought of herself as glass, but having to rely on Brayden had just told her what she was.

Weak.

Needy.

"Stop thinking so hard, Ally," Brayden whispered in her ear, the warm tendrils of his breath sending shivers of need down her spine, a need she didn't want to acknowledge.

"I'm not thinking hard," she countered.

"Yes, you are." He pulled back and rubbed a finger down the middle of her eyebrows to the tip of her nose. "You get this little line right here when you're thinking about things that make you sad or angry. I know it's there; I don't need to see it."

"Stop knowing me so well, Brayden Cooper."

"I know you better than I know myself, Ally. Just because I haven't acted on it doesn't mean I don't know you. I didn't act on it because, at first, I couldn't, and then later, it was too soon. Yeah, I know three years seems like forever, but I wanted to make sure you were ready. I know what makes you smile, what makes you ache. I know it all."

Her heart swelled at his words even though she begged it not to. "I don't know how that's possible."

He framed her face and kissed her lips. "I love you, Ally. I've always loved you. I just didn't say it. It's funny that my family thought I didn't know my own feelings. But I've always known, Ally. Always."

She let out a breath. "I'm bad for you, Bray. Greg's parents aren't going to forget their goal. They want my babies because of the blood that runs through their veins, but I'm not going to let that happen."

"I'm not going to let that happen either. Those kids are part of you, part of me. Just because they don't have my name doesn't mean I don't consider them mine."

This was all happening too fast. His words meant promises that she wasn't sure she could keep. Just because he thought he wanted it all now didn't mean he'd want it later. Though she trusted him far more than she'd ever trusted Greg, that didn't mean she could do it fully. She couldn't let her children's hearts be broken over him. She couldn't let her own heart be broken either.

But, then she remembered the look on Brayden's face while he held Lacy close. It was already too late to rein in their little minds and hearts. It was already too late to rein in her own.

She'd already told him she loved him. She'd already given herself to him in all but her body, and she knew that would come.

Soon.

Why was she holding herself back? Why was she letting these doubts attack her when they weren't worth it? She wasn't the type to live in the moment, but it would be nice to do so, even for a second.

"Ally?"

She shook her head then laid it on his chest, his heart beating beneath her ear like a lifeline.

"I'm okay. At least now."

"I don't want you to leave. I know David's gone, but the danger isn't over. I want you and the kids to stay."

"Of course," she said easily, though the disappointment settled in at the cold practically of the reasons forcing them to stay.

He pushed her back and framed her face again. "I want you to stay for so many more reasons than protection. I never want you to leave, but I think it's too early for me to say that. So, for now, I'll lie and say I want you to stay only because of the dangers out there and not because I love you and Aiden, Lacy, and

Cameron like my own family, like my everything. I won't tell you that I want you to stay because I want us to be together in every future I can see."

Allison stared into his eyes, and her heart beat faster. She loved him far more than she should. But because she couldn't think past keeping her kids safe, she'd put his promises aside and keep them for later.

She couldn't think of herself; her family was more important.

But his words would keep her warm when she couldn't think past the world coming down around her.

"Brayden..."

"No, don't say anything. I don't want to hear it. Let's go downstairs and talk to Tyler before he leaves. The kids are in bed, and then it will just be you and me. And there *will* be a you and me, Ally."

She didn't say a word as they walked hand in hand to the living room where Tyler sat in front of a fire, his arm around Abby. The other Coopers had gone home after they'd let the Malones settle, not wanting to crowd them.

Tyler had called the ME to take care of David's body, citing a hiking accident rather than telling the truth. He'd even interviewed some people who couldn't remember anything unusual happening on the playground meaning David's magic must have worked better than they'd hoped. She'd never thought of herself as bloodthirsty, but she'd almost been sorry that none of them had helped him over the ledge.

He'd hurt her babies. The image of ropes around Lacy's wrists would never leave her mind.

When Allison and Brayden reached the living room, Tyler's head rose. The steel glint in his eyes would normally have scared her, but this time, it gave her comfort. He was a Cooper, one of the few who cared for her and her family. They sat down across from Tyler and Abby, and tension radiated through Allison.

She didn't want to talk to them about what had happened. Didn't want to remember the lifeless look on David's face at the bottom of the cliff. Didn't want to think about how she'd try to explain it to her children again, knowing they were too old for lies and make believe. Though they lived in a town full of fairy tales and myths, the realistic truths of death and hatred were there and had to be dealt with.

"The kids asleep?" Tyler asked, his voice low.

"Thankfully," Allison answered. "I'm surprised they could even sleep after what happened today." Her voice caught at that, but she swallowed her fear—it wouldn't do any good now to weep and scream at the unfairness of it all. She also knew that, though her babies were sleeping now, it didn't mean they would in the future. She'd prepared herself for the nightmares as best as she could.

Just not her own.

"That's good," Tyler said. "I want you to be able to get to sleep soon, so I'll be quick. We recovered David's body." She flinched, but

Tyler was kind enough to ignore it and continue on. "Everyone thinks it was a hiking accident, and there's no trace of what happened to Lacy or Aiden. It kills me to have to lie like this, and frankly, I'm not sure I did the right thing. I have to uphold the law. It's my job, but I also know that things aren't black and white anymore, and we have to protect our secrets."

Allison nodded, bile rising in her throat.

"I'd rather protect your children, Ally," Tyler reasoned. "That's why I called the North Pole." He let out a snort. "Never thought I'd say that, but things are changing. Up there they know how to clean things up and what to do in these situations. Though they don't have to hide it up there, they have to hide it from the rest of the world. I also talked with a few of the elves about forming a special police force here in Holiday. One that will deal with magical matters since we seem to have more issues with that now. I know you don't want to hear about this now, but I wanted you to know that things will be different. At least as different as I can make them. We're going to have a plan and a way of protecting ourselves and our secrets."

Brayden muttered under his breath and tightened his hold on her. She leaned into him, not caring that she was doing exactly what she said she wouldn't do—relying on someone other than herself.

This was Brayden.

He was different.

And he wanted her.

Maybe she could lean on him...just for a little bit.

She bit back a curse. That wasn't fair to either of them, and frankly, this wasn't the time to be thinking about it.

"Okay," she finally said.

Tyler's mouth hitched up in a half smile, and he kissed Abby's temple. "I know it's a lot to think about right now, but I wanted to let you know just the same. Now, about the things that concern you."

She bit her lip, and Brayden tightened his hold again. God, she loved this man, even though she knew she shouldn't.

"What is it, Tyler?" Brayden asked.

"We know David wasn't working alone, and he said as much. I looked up what I could about the grandparents, and they seem to be staying where they are. The authorities there are letting them know of David's demise, which might set them off. Rina told us all she could about gnomes, and I'm still a little wary of what they could do."

Allison nodded, understanding.

They weren't safe.

They couldn't be safe with Greg's parents out there.

"She's going to stay here with me. The kids too," Brayden said in that quiet way of his, and Allison immediately relaxed and wanted to tense at the same time.

Who was he to order them about?

Brayden looked down at her and raised a brow. "Is that okay with you?"

Oh, great, now he takes my opinion into account?

She couldn't put her own issues at the forefront, not when she had Aiden, Cameron, and Lacy to think about.

And, God, she wanted to stay for far more reasons than safety. She wanted to stay because she loved him. Loved the way he cared for her and her children, loved the way he made her feel and smile. Yes, she wanted to stay, but she wouldn't tell him that—couldn't tell him that. Not when the emotions running through her were so chaotic she didn't know what she was thinking anymore.

"Yes, that works for me. The kids love staying here anyway."

At the word love, something brightened in Brayden's gaze, but neither of them mentioned her use of the word love. They had a lot to talk about that couldn't be said in front of Tyler and Abby.

As if sensing the undercurrents in their conversation, Abby stood quickly and dragged Tyler up with her.

"It's settled then. All of us will be around when we can," Abby explained. "Just stay safe, and we'll make a plan to protect everyone. I know this sucks right now, but we're moving forward."

Allison nodded, and they said their goodbyes. Soon she was left in a cooling foyer with Brayden, and she didn't know if she wanted to jump into his arms and never let go or run to her guest room and hide until she could think straight.

Frankly, she didn't know when that time could come as it was.

"Ally?"

She turned to find Brayden closer than she'd thought. She could smell the earthy scent that drew her toward him every time she saw him. Allison closed her eyes and inhaled, needing that steadiness that came when she knew he was there—even as her heart raced at the thought of being alone with him.

They'd danced around each other for so long and had started the process of becoming something more than just friends who felt tingles around each other. Now it was time to at least start to make sense of the mess they'd made.

There was no way she'd be able to go to sleep without knowing at least if there was a direction for them to go at all.

They loved each other, but she wasn't sure she could trust it.

That just made her angrier. It wasn't Brayden's fault that she'd been hurt far more than physically in the past. It wasn't his fault that she couldn't trust.

She took a deep breath and took a step closer. His eyes widened, but he stood stock-still, as if he knew she could bolt at any moment.

It wasn't his fault she was afraid.

It wasn't.

"Thank you, Brayden. For everything."

"You don't have to thank me. You know I'd do anything for you." She watched as he struggled for control then gave in, tracing a finger down her arm, sending shivers in its wake.

Allison tilted her head up, catching his gaze. She could stare into those ocean-blue eyes for days, always finding something new and exciting. Why had she been holding herself back from him?

"Brayden..."

"Don't say anything you don't mean, Ally. I don't want you to run away because you're scared, and I don't want you to come closer if you feel grateful." He slid his palms down her back then up, catching the edge of her shirt, his fingertips, calloused from working with his hands, rough on her smooth skin. "I want you in my arms, in my bed, and in my life because you want to be, not because you feel you need to pay me back."

"It would never be like that, Bray. You know I love you. We've both said the words and thought about the future. We both know that it could end badly. That's why we've been afraid."

He gripped her chin so she couldn't avoid his gaze. "No, that's why you've been afraid. I've been afraid to hurt you, not seeing what was in front of my face the whole time. I thought you didn't want me, didn't want to be with me. Yeah, I stood back because I was waiting for the right time and never knew when that was, but I didn't know if you'd want me. You didn't show anything to me that said love in the past. That's why I stood back these past couple years, but I'm not standing back anymore, Ally. Once I get you in my bed and in my life, I'm not letting you go. So, I'm going to give you this choice. I'm not going to force you there, but once you're there, I'm not going to let you leave."

Though his high-handedness should have scared her, but right then, it made her want him more—something totally opposite of what it usually was. She knew that it would be her decision to let him in close, just as it was his decision to want to keep her—as much as she'd want to keep him.

Could she trust it?

That was something she'd have to have faith in. She'd spent her whole life doing what others wanted of her, never letting go... Maybe it was time to be free and hold tight to what she wanted.

"I don't know if I want you to let me go, Bray. But, I'm here now. Can that be enough?"

He shook his head then ran kisses down her brow, her cheek, her jaw. "No, it's not enough. But I don't believe you. I don't think you're going to go. I might be the stupidest man you've ever seen by going with my gut and my luck rather than your words, but I'm taking you, Ally."

His voice, low and ready, mixed with the softness of his lips on her skin made her thighs clench, aching for him. She was no stranger to sex. No, she'd had three kids and let—no, had *endured*—Greg keep her down for years, but she knew it would be different with Brayden.

She *needed* it to be different with Brayden.

"I'm going to try my best." She just hoped it was good enough.

He stared at her for a few moments as if searching for an answer that she hadn't given. She lifted her chin from his hold but didn't look anywhere but his face, his high cheekbones and his strong jaw.

Finally, he nodded then lowered his lips. He tasted of mint, coffee, and that thing that was just Brayden. She melted into him, deepening his kiss. God, she needed him. Needed this.

He nipped at her lips, her tongue, tasting her while she did the same to him. Finally, he pulled back, his pupils wide, just a little bit of blue around the edges. Both of them panted heavily, knowing this was the start of something more...something they would finish tonight.

"My children..."

"Are asleep and tucked in their beds."

"But what if they wake up?"

"Then they'll find you in my room, though the door will be locked. They're old enough to know that I love you, Ally. I think Aiden is even old enough to know that something is going on with us."

She filed that information for later as she'd have to talk to all her children about this, even if only in general without details. She wouldn't go in blind—she couldn't.

He tugged at her hand, and she followed him willingly up the stars, past her room to the master bedroom.

He had decorated with strong, dark furniture, deep green colors that seemed to go with his leprechaun and luck, and had candles lit.

"Candles?"

She could have sworn a blush rose to his cheeks as he shrugged it off.

"I lit them when you were putting Lacy to bed. I wanted to make it special for you, Ally."

Touched, she walked to him and slid her arms around his neck. "It would have been special even without the candles, Bray. I don't need silk and promises. I just need you."

"I'm not a sweet man, Ally." She opened her mouth to say just the opposite, but he cut her off. "No, I'm not. I'll do anything anyone needs of me outside of here, but in this room, in my bed, you're mine. I don't want to share you with anyone, not even in your thoughts. I'm going to take all I can and give everything and more right back. I'm not going to be gentle in here, and I don't want to be. I'll make it the best we can, and I'll try not to scare you, but it's taking all that I am not to throw you down on your stomach and sink into you from behind over and over again until you're panting my name."

Her breath caught in her throat at his words and the images they created in her head. God, she didn't know he could be this way...with this edge. She liked it. It wasn't anything like Greg, and she wanted more. She buried the thought of her dead husband as soon as it came up. It wasn't the time for memories of that man; he'd had his.

Now she'd have hers.

"I want it all, Bray. I'm not afraid of you. I could never be. Just tell me what to do, and I'm yours."

He smiled then, a truly feral smile. He turned from her then, and before she could taste the disappointment, she heard the click of the lock on the door, and he was on her. His mouth took hers with a burning force, demanding more than she thought she had. She kissed back with the same intensity, their teeth clashing, their bodies brushing against each other. This wouldn't be a soft, innocent first love. No, this would be a hard, pounding, sweaty turn in the sheets. She'd give so much of her heart and her love, but she'd take so much more in return.

Brayden pulled back first, and she felt cold at the loss, stupid she knew. He pulled off his shirt in a quick motion, his chest and abs rippling as he did so. She reached out to touch him, needing to feel his heat, but he put a hand on her wrists.

"Not yet."

"But—"

He shook his head, cutting her off. "No, not yet. I'm going to touch every inch of you, taste you, and lick you. Then, once you've come on my face and my hand, you can touch me as I sink into that pussy of yours."

Her eyes widened at the brazen words, but then she smiled. "Bring it."

He threw his head back and laughed. "I'm glad you're not one of those weeping, fainting gals."

She raised a brow. "Been with many of those, have you?"

He just grinned. "Oh no, I know better than to mention anyone else but you when I'm about to fill you with my cock. There's no one before this, Ally. No one after."

She didn't say anything at his promise, just looked down his toned body to the cock he mentioned, straining at his zipper. Oh, how she yearned to relieve him of that ache and wrap her lips around the whole of him.

"I like where your thoughts are going, Ally-mine. And soon I'll let you get on your knees while I fuck that pretty mouth."

"Let?"

"Let. You'll want it."

"I thought you were the sweet Cooper," she teased. "What's with the dirty mouth?"

His eyes darkened, not in the anger she'd grown to expect from other men but in the heat she knew was only him. "I keep telling everyone I'm not the nice one. That's Matt and now Justin. I'm going to say any crude thing that comes to mind as I pound into that pussy of yours, and we're both going to like it. Then when we're sated a long, long time from now, I'll say the sweet words we both mean, and I'm not letting you go." Even as he said it, he moved to the other side of the room, leaving space that seemed to go on forever.

"I love you, Brayden." She needed to say it now before he went dark and she let him fade away. She needed to make sure he knew as much as she needed to remember it.

He smiled, happiness edging out the darkness that came with his demands. "I love you, too, Ally-mine. Now I'm going to strip you down, inch by inch, then taste you."

She shivered at his words and spread her arms, ready. He prowled toward her. There was no other word for it. He moved smoothly, graceful as a cat as he came to her and tugged on her shirt. She raised her arms as he slid it over her head. The room was heated so she knew the goose bumps that rose on her flesh weren't from the cold, but from his nearness.

He traced her arms, even as his breath caught when his gaze reached her breasts, full but not as high as they'd been before three kids. She knew he could see the slight stretch marks on her stomach and hips, but she didn't care. Not with the way he looked at her now.

Brayden's fingertips slid across her raised marks and smiled. "You're beautiful."

"You're full of it."

He shook his head then knelt before her, his lips coming in contact with her stomach, stretch marks and all. "What do women call these?" he murmured. "Oh yeah, badges of honor. You got these from bringing three of the best kids a man could ask for into this world. They're a part of you, so they make you beautiful."

Touched, she ran a hand through his hair.

He looked up and narrowed his eyes. "What did I say about touching?" he said as he nipped at her then roughly stripped her out of her jeans. She reached behind her to grip the armchair so she wouldn't fall. She knew better than to touch him now.

And, oh, God, she loved it.

Without words, he kissed down her belly, her legs, tracing his tongue along the seam of her panties, licking just beneath the edge.

She rubbed her legs together, needing him to touch her clit and make her come. She'd never had a man do that for her. Only her own hand had ever brought her to that point. But she had a feeling Brayden would know exactly what to do.

He pulled her legs apart then, still knelling before her as she stood in her bra and panties. He pressed his face against her core and nibbled at her through the cloth, and her body shuddered.

Damn, this man was so hot.

And he was hers.

She could scarcely believe it.

Before she could think more, he gripped her panties and tugged hard, the elastic ripping.

"Brayden."

"Shh," he said as he threw the tattered remains of her underwear across the room and bared her pussy to his face. He slid his fingers through the curls, and she blushed.

She should have shaved for him, but for some reason, she didn't care right now, needing him to touch her more.

"You're beautiful."

Allison shook her head. "Not really, I've gone through three births, Brayden. I'm...I'm different."

"You're mine," he growled. He spread her lower lips, leaning in and nipping here and there. She leaned back until her bottom touched the chair. "Sit, Ally. Let me taste you."

She blushed again but did as she was told. When she sat, he scooted closer and spread her legs, leaving her bare to him. He blew cold air against her heat, sending shivers down her spine.

"Brayden, please."

"Oh, I will, Ally-mine. I will." He traced his finger along her swollenness then circled her clit but didn't press.

Damn.

His finger continued its path until he entered her and curled his finger, finding that one place she didn't think existed.

"Brayden..."

He smiled then leaned down, letting his tongue continue the exploration his finger had just finished as he let another finger join the first. He licked and sucked on her clit, her body heating and rolling, and she was sure her pussy was wetter than it had ever been. He pumped into her, adding a third, a fourth finger, then he bit down, and she came. Hard.

She bucked against his face as he kept moving, bringing more out of her. Allison laid her head against the back of the chair, flushed, and still needy for him. She'd never come that hard before, not even with her own hand.

"Can I touch you now?"

Whose deep, sultry voice was that? Surely not hers.

"Let me play with those breasts of yours, taste each nipple until they're red and ready to be plucked, then you can touch me."

Jesus, this man would be the death of her. But, oh, God, what a way to go.

Brayden stood up and unclasped the back of her bra, her breasts falling, heavy, ready.

"They're not as high as they used to be..." She bit her lip, ashamed she wasn't the perky twenty-year-old he could have had.

He shook his head. "Get it through that head of yours, Ally-mine. I love you, every inch of you. These breasts are perfect." He lifted one in each hand and brought them to his mouth one by one. His tongue circled her nipple, and she felt herself get wet all over again as her pussy throbbed right along with her breasts.

"These breasts taste like perfection, Ally-mine. They're you, so they're everything I need. Okay, baby?"

She looked into his gaze and nodded. He wasn't saying pretty words so he could have her. No, he said what he meant, and she loved him all the more for it.

"Okay, but can I touch you now?"

He laughed then rolled her nipple in his fingers, harder than she was used to, but she liked it. The slight pain sent tingles down her body, and she arched into him. Brayden was different but hers, and she wanted what he did...at least for the moment.

She gasped as he bit down on her nipple.

"Stop thinking, Ally-mine. Just feel."

She smiled down at him, liking his pet name for her and how he saw through her.

He sucked on her breasts again as his hand slid down her belly and found her clit. He tweaked and played with her, knowing exactly how to press into her until she came, biting his shoulder so she didn't scream his name and wake the children.

Brayden chuckled and kissed her. "Bite as hard as you want, Ally-mine."

"I need you, Brayden." She gasped, surprising herself that she could even want to come again.

"Let me get a condom."

She nodded then staggered to the bed, her legs weak from the orgasms she didn't know could be so intense.

Ally heard the crinkle of foil then looked over as he wrapped his cock.

"Dear God," she whispered.

He threw his head back and laughed. "Brayden, Ally-mine. My name is Brayden."

"Oh, shut up," she shot back as she blushed. She hadn't meant to say the first part aloud, but dear God, the man was freaking huge. He was long, but not too long. But, where he really shined was in width. She wasn't sure he was going to fit. She blushed at the thought of him trying. Oh, it'd be worth it.

He smiled a truly male smile and climbed up so he lay between her legs. "Glad you like it."

"You've been hiding that in your pants all this time? It's a wonder you haven't walked with a limp."

He shook his head and teased her entrance, the wide head probing, throbbing. "I do what I can. Now keep those eyes open, Ally-mine. I want to see you when I take you."

"Hard, Brayden. I'm not some weak-kneed virgin. I want to feel all of you."

His eyes darkened, and he entered her in one thrust. He froze when she called out, pleasure and pain wrapping around her in a macabre beauty as he filled her more than she thought possible. They were connected in every way that mattered, more than anything.

"Ally?"

"Move," she gasped. "You're mine, Brayden."

"You're mine, Ally." He pulled back then flexed his hips, reaching a demanding rhythm, hitting her G-spot with each thrust, sparks starting behind her eyelids. She opened her eyes, knowing she needed to see him as he came. For a moment she wanted him to take off the condom so she could feel all of him and have him fill her with his cum, but she refrained, knowing there would be time in the future for that.

He pounded into her, and her nails raked down his back as she fought back a scream. Sweat dripped down his face and chest as he rotated his hips and hit her in a new, heated spot. The cords on the side of his neck flexed, and he cursed.

"Come, Ally-mine, come. I can't hold back much longer."

She nodded, unable to speak as she let herself go over that peak, and watched the pleasure in his eyes, and he followed her.

"Brayden," she finally whispered as he leaned on her, their bodies still connected, his cock still throbbing. She inhaled his scent and frowned.

Smoke?

Why did he smell of smoke?

She looked around and froze.

"Oh, fuck," Brayden said as he pulled out of her. She winced. "We knocked over a fucking candle." He took a blanket and put out the small flame and fell back laughing, tears running down his cheeks.

She joined him then and forced her body to move so she straddled him. Brayden traced a finger down her face and smiled.

"We set the sheets on fire," he finally said.

"In more ways than one," she added.

They kissed and held each other as they lay in the smoke-filled room for a bit more. She knew they'd have to get up soon and deal with the mess and then the feelings that were just as messy within her. But, for now, she'd be content to lie in his arms and know that there might be a future. As scared as she was to admit it, she wanted that future more than anything.

If only things were that easy.

Chapter 9

Brayden watched as Lacy ran through Jackson's room, Cameron hot on her tail. It'd been almost a week since everything had happened, and the kids had bounced back stronger than ever. It could have been from the fact that they had the Coopers around them now, but Brayden wasn't sure.

They'd all come to Jackson's for the weekly Cooper dinner, and Justin was in the kitchen cooking with Abby and Rina. Tyler and Jackson were outside dealing with something Jacks wanted Matt to build later while Matt himself was most likely locked in a closet somewhere with Jordan. They appeared to be trying to start a family considering how often he found them tangled in an embrace meant for behind closed doors.

Though they were all still learning to live together, and danger still lurked, the arrangement seemed to be working. The kids went to school with a set of Cooper eyes on them at all times. It wasn't the best solution, but it seemed to be working for now. Since all three kids could see through the magic of a gnome, they knew to run to the nearest Cooper if they thought something was wrong. They were never to be alone if they could help it, and by living with Brayden, they at least had some security.

Allison's dumbass landlord had changed the locks since she'd brought "trouble" to the place. They could have fought it, and Tyler was ready to, but Allison had given in—much to Brayden's delight. She'd mumbled something about finding another place when necessary, but he didn't care. She was living with him, and that was all that mattered.

She still worked at the diner and he at his shop, so he couldn't be around her twenty-four hours a day, but he took what he could.

He loved the woman with every inch of his soul, and he wasn't going to let her go without a fight.

Lacy ran past again, this time running into a table and almost falling. Brayden reached out to steady her, and she laughed it off before running in the opposite direction.

"Don't run in the house," Allison admonished as she came to his side. He wrapped an arm around her waist easily, and she leaned into him.

He held back a relived sigh that she'd come to him almost unconsciously. They'd only really been together for a week, though she'd slept in his bed every night. He wouldn't have it any other way. Their public displays had gone a bit slower than he'd like. A few touches here, a casual kiss there. But, once he locked the bedroom door, he had her in every way possible—on every piece of furniture he owned. He'd have to find a few new pieces to add to the room so he could see what she tasted like from every angle.

As if she could hear what he was thinking—which could be a possibility considered his cock ached like a son of a bitch—she pulled back, giving him space. He wanted to curse, but he knew it was because of the kids in the room. She still wasn't comfortable with his love; it was as if she didn't completely trust it. Though he couldn't fault her for it, it still pissed him off to no end.

Lacy and Cameron seemed to take their relationship in stride, Lacy especially, as she considered living with him and having him near every day her due. Cameron just enjoyed the fact that he had someone new to play with that would always be there.

Aiden, on the other hand, could pose a problem.

Brayden looked over Allison's shoulder to her oldest son, who didn't quite glare, but eyed them thoughtfully. It was past time he and the boy had a talk. Aiden's feelings, whatever they may be, weren't his fault. But, Brayden needed to step up and talk to the oldest man in the house, to make sure Aiden knew he wasn't going anywhere.

Why did the thought of talking to a twelve-year-old scare him more than anything?

Oh, yeah, the kid held his future in his hands. The kid *was* his future. He just needed to make sure Aiden knew that.

He felt more than saw Allison following his gaze then tensing.

"Brayden," she said as she sighed away from him.

"I'll take care of it. Aiden and I need to talk anyway."

"Maybe I shouldn't be here."

He leaned down and stole a kiss. She blushed but glared. "Don't stress. This is a man-to-man talk. I've already talked to Cam and Lacy, but this one needs to be done now before we move on. I won't hurt him."

She shook her head and grabbed his hand. "I never thought you would."

Relief filled him at the thought she trusted him at least that little bit. He walked toward Aiden. The boy raised his chin, but it didn't deter him.

"Hey, Aid, let's talk."

Aiden flinched then grumbled, "I don't know what we have to talk about."

Fuck.

Brayden knew he should have talked to Aiden before this but had put it off because he was a coward.

"Come on, we need to," Brayden said, his voice carefully light.

Aiden looked over at Allison, who gave a nod. "Fine."

"Okay then. Let's go out to the backyard."

Aiden didn't say anything as they walked past Tyler and Jackson, who were walking in with raised brows. Brayden shook his head, knowing he'd have to talk to his brothers sooner or later.

Preferably later.

He grabbed a couple of jackets on the peg near the back door, knowing that one would be too big for Aiden, but any jacket would do right now. They pulled them on, Brayden struggling not to help Aiden with his. He remembered what it felt like to be a twelve-year-old boy on the verge of being a man—at least in a kid's eyes. And with what they had to talk about, Brayden wasn't sure Aiden would want any form of his help anyway.

"What did you want to talk about?" Aiden grumbled, his chin raised.

Brayden let out a breath. This wasn't going to be easy, but it had to be done. He loved this kid like his own, and Aiden had to realize that.

"I think you know, Aid."

Aiden kicked a stone, his gaze on something Brayden couldn't see.

"I don't know what I think."

"Then let's talk about it." Brayden moved to stand by Aiden, careful to leave space and not touch him.

They stood there for a few moments before Brayden spoke, "I'm sorry everything's changing so fast for you."

Aiden shrugged, then stood there in silence.

"Aiden?"

"Were you friends with us—I mean me, Cam, and Lacy—just to get with my mom?" Aiden asked.

Shocked, Brayden turned to the little boy who'd stolen his heart. "What? How could you say that?"

Aiden shrugged. "Because you never used to talk to Mom the way you do. You never used to kiss her. And I know you sleep in the same bed and everything. You just want her for sex."

"What do you know about that?" Brayden asked, suddenly feeling like a fish out of water. What did he know about kids? Everything he'd thought he'd known was superficial. He was in some dangerous territory here.

Jesus, what did twelve-year-olds know about sex these days? Maybe he should have had Allison come out with him.

"I know enough," he growled, his arms above his chest. "I know you and Mom sleep in the same bed. You'll probably make new babies and leave us alone. Then you'll take Mom away and hit her like Dad did. I'm not going to let you do that, you know. You don't get to have Mom. She's ours. I couldn't stop Dad when he hit her before, but I'll stop you."

Tears ran down Aiden's cheeks, but Brayden made sure he didn't point them out. He also stopped himself from doing what he really wanted to do—hug Aiden tight and take away the nightmares.

"Aiden, I'm not going to hit your mom or any of you." No longer able to resist, Brayden leaned down so they were eye level. "I don't know everything your dad did, but I'm not like him. You've known me all your life, and you know what I could or couldn't do."

"Yeah, you say that now. But if my dad can do all that, what says you can't too?"

"Because I love you guys. I'm not going to hurt you. Hitting is wrong. No matter how angry you and your mom could make me—which wouldn't be that angry since you guys pretty much rock—I'd never lay a hand on you. I don't talk with my fists."

Aiden sniffed and wiped his cheeks. "Whatever."

"No, not whatever. I love you guys. I want us to be a family. I wasn't your friend before so I could get in with your mom. I was your friend... no, I *am* your friend because I like you, Cam, and Lacy. You guys stole my heart as much as your mom did. And when your mom lets it happen, I'm going marry her. When I do that, I'll marry the three of you as well. I want us all together in my big house for more than just protection. I want us together because we mean something together."

Aiden stared at him a long time before he said anything. "So you'll be my dad?"

Brayden swallowed hard, determined not to fall on his knees and cry. "If that's what you want to call me. I'll be anything you want, but I want to be your family. I want you to have uncles and aunts who love you, and I want you to be okay with the fact that I love your mom."

"I don't know." He shifted from foot to foot, but looked a bit more relaxed.

"Aiden, I don't know the complete story of what your dad did. I know some of it, but I know there's more out there. If you ever want to talk about it, I'm here."

Aiden sniffed again. "Is it bad that I'm happy he's gone?"

Brayden scratched his chin. "No. Some people might say differently, but in my opinion, if a man could do what he did, then you can be glad he's not in your life anymore. And I'm not Greg, Aid. I'll take care of you, and I won't hit you. I might get mad a couple times if we don't see eye to eye or if you're mean to your mom, but I'll never take my anger out on you. I know you can't believe me on my word alone since you've had trust broken by another, but I'm determined to show you that you can trust me. Okay?"

"You really love my mom?"

A little seed of hope filled him. "With everything I am. Though I love you three just as much—just a bit differently."

Aiden smiled, and Brayden felt as though he'd won every contest and game out there.

"You'll take care of her, right? Because I try, but sometimes she still thinks I'm a little kid and won't let me help."

Damn, he was about to melt into a puddle of gooey cheesiness right there and love this kid more than anything.

"So are we okay?" he asked.

"Yeah. When are you going to marry Mom?"

Brayden chuckled. "When she lets me. But if I have your blessing, I think that'll help matters."

Aiden bit his lip and looked like he was thinking hard before he smiled. "Okay. Just as long as you get flowers. She likes those."

"Right, thanks for the advice, kid."

Brayden threw his arm over Aiden's shoulders, pleased he didn't flinch like he had in the past few weeks, and walked back to the house where Allison stood on the porch, her arms wrapped around herself and her teeth nibbling on her lip.

"Is everything okay, boys?"

Brayden looked down at Aiden and nodded. "Sure is."

Allison didn't look convinced so he reached out and pulled her to him, letting his lips brush hers.

"Love you," he whispered.

Allison pulled back, wide eyed, then looked down at Aiden, who was smiling. "Love you too."

Hell, yeah, Brayden thought. One step closer to that family he wanted.

He wrapped his other arm around her waist and led them back into the house. He and Aiden took off their borrowed jackets, and Brayden let the warmth of the room seep into him. Though it was already mid-March, the weather hadn't warmed up enough for his tastes. Montana liked its cold and sometimes refused to let go until well into the summer.

"Food's ready," Justin said as he popped his head into the living room. "And it's delicious if I do say so myself."

Brayden rolled his eyes. "Yeah, and how much of that chicken did you swipe before you put it on the table?"

Justin gaped. "Who me? Like I'd ever steal food before people got a chance to taste it."

"Then how did you know it was delicious?" Cameron asked as he ran up to Justin.

Brayden snorted. "Yeah, Justin, how?"

Justin narrowed his eyes then shook his head. "Oh, I see how it is. You get your kids to gang up on me."

When he left the room, Brayden let that settle on him. *His* kids. Damn, he liked the sound of that. He looked down at Allison and smiled at the confusion on her face. Oh, she was outnumbered now, and for some reason, he liked it. He just had to make sure she knew he wasn't leaving her life, no matter what happened.

They all sat around the table, much more crowded than it used to be. Everyone but Jackson had a woman with them, and Brayden had brought three kids to the table. They'd all grown these past few months, though he knew changes were still coming.

As they were about to eat, the phone rang, and Jackson tensed. Brayden looked at his eldest brother like he was crazy. He knew Jacks didn't like interruptions, but the tension on his face didn't look like annoyance. No, he looked scared.

Matt sat the closest so he stood up and answered. "Hello?"

Matt frowned, and Brayden got a bad feeling.

"No, you can't talk to them. No, I don't think so."

Brayden stood quickly as Allison turned to him, her eyes wide. He ran a hand down her neck and reached Matt's side, as whoever was on the line apparently hung up on him.

"Who was it?" Brayden demanded.

Matt clenched his jaw and looked over Brayden's shoulder. "We'll talk about it later."

"Kids, can you go upstairs and play with my new Xbox for a bit?" Jackson asked.

Aiden, Cameron, and Lacy looked toward Allison, who gave a small nod. They left the room, though it was clear from their faces that they wanted to stay.

"Was it Greg's parents?" Allison asked.

Matt nodded. "They just called to threaten us saying they'd find a way to get the children. Nothing we didn't already know. I know I should have probably given you the phone, but I didn't want you to have to deal with them in front of your children."

Allison nodded, and Brayden walked back to grip her hand.

"We'll deal with this, Ally."

She shook her head. "When will it stop? We can't just keep hiding and trying to make things better. We're all scared, and this is ridiculous."

Brayden knelt and framed her face. "We're not going to let them win, Ally. They're just saying words. I know they have magic and can make us do things, but the kids can see through it, and I'm pretty sure my luck can help us. Me and my brothers can fight off their magic for some reason. Yes, they can do things physically and mentally to others, but we can fight them, baby."

"Your luck? What has it helped so far?" She narrowed her eyes at him but it didn't mask the fear.

Brayden let her lash out at him. She didn't have anyone else to focus her anger on, and she needed to let go.

"It helped us find Aiden and then Lacy; I know it did."

She let out a breath. "I know, Bray. I'm sorry."

He kissed her softly, aware his brothers and the girls were watching. "Yell at me all you want. I'm not letting you or the kids get hurt."

"What I don't understand is why the cops can't get involved," Justin finally said.

Tyler shook his head. "We can get the verbal threats on record, but it won't do anything. They haven't done anything else wrong." He held up his hand as Brayden and Allison opened their mouths to object. "No, they haven't. At least nothing we can prove. And, because we had to avoid discussing magic, David's part in all of this isn't even clear. Yeah, it sucks, but there's nothing we can do but make sure we keep watch."

"But we can't do it twenty-four hours a day," Allison said as she leaned into Brayden.

He kissed her temple and rubbed her back. "We'll find a way."

"This sucks," Jordan said, and the rest of the people around the table let out small chuckles.

"Pretty much," Allison agreed. "I'm going to have to take them somewhere else, somewhere we can hide."

Pain hit him hard, his breath quickening. "No, that won't help anything," he said once he caught his breath.

Allison looked at him through tear filled eyes. "I know."

Aiden, Cameron, and Lacy came down soon after, and everyone ate a subdued dinner. Not even Justin and Matt's jokes could keep the conversation rolling.

Why couldn't he fix this for them? What was the point of being gifted with luck if he couldn't help the ones he loved?

He could make money in any investment, find a lucky penny, miss a step but not fall, make a rainbow to watch Lacy smile, but he couldn't keep the demons away.

Gnomes had a magic that could blind a person from what was really happening, they could also control and paralyze them, and he had nothing to fight that. He could keep up with security and pray his luck would hold, but would it be enough?

He didn't know how far his Cooper blood would hold, but he wouldn't tell Allison that. No, he needed to keep her safe and he knew she already had the same thoughts as he did.

He wasn't sure Allison thought it was. No, he was sure she didn't. He had a feeling she might run and take them with her, leaving him all alone with just his coin and memories that wouldn't fade.

Jesus, these gnomes wanted her—no, *their*—children, and there wasn't anything he could do.

The law was on their side, but that didn't matter to people like the Malones. At least the Malones that were full gnome.

Soon it was time to leave, and he didn't want to let Allison go back to her place—back to her old life. He wouldn't let that happen.

"Hey, guys, we're going to take the kids to our place," Jordan said as she wrapped an arm around Cameron's shoulder.

Allison shook her head. "No, I can't impose. Plus I don't want them out of my sight."

Jordan snapped her fingers, and a ball of light sparked from her fingertips. "See this? Well, that's just a taste of my power. When I get going, I can create fire, wind, and use any of the other elements."

"What about the gnomes power?" Allison asked.

Rina shook her head. "The only ones that can protect themselves one hundred percent are the kids themselves because they are gnomes too. But we're all a little bit magic." She glanced at Jackson, Matt, and Allison. "Well, most of us. That gives us some immunity. And, frankly, the way you talked Brayden about what happened at the caves, I'm thinking with all the powers being granted to you guys recently, I'm thinking you're immune."

Brayden sat back and thought about it. "I barely felt the magic wash over me. I don't think it was because of my coin either because it didn't heat up. It must be because we're Coopers. After all, we've stood through so much together as it is."

His brothers grunted in approval.

"Great, I'm the only one who can't help," Allison grumbled.

He kissed her brow. "You're their mom. You're everything to them. Don't forget that."

Jordan cleared her throat and continued. "I'm not going to let anything happen to them. I think you and Bray need some time to talk. Plus, Matt and I want to practice our skills with kids." She blushed, and Matt came up from behind her, Lacy in his arms, and kissed her cheek.

"Yeah, and why not practice on already made kids?" He laughed then tickled Lacy, who giggled.

Allison shifted from foot to foot before nodding, hugging them goodbye, and telling them to be good. Relief filled Brayden at the thought of being alone with her. They needed time with just the two of them, and Matt and Jordan had given them the opportunity. From the look on Matt's face, Brayden knew that there'd be payback in the future. No issue there since he owed his family more than he could ever hope to repay after all they'd done to protect his new family.

By the time they made it back to his house, Allison looked as though she wanted to turn right around and get her babies.

"Ally, it will be okay."

She smiled and took off her jacket. "Don't get me wrong, I trust Matt and Jordan. I mean, I wouldn't allow this if I didn't. But that doesn't mean I'm not worried. I don't know what Greg's parents are going to do."

He stepped toward her and framed her face. "Well, there's nothing they can do right now. Tyler's keeping an eye on them as best as he can from here using his contacts in their police force, and they can't legally do anything at all. I know they can try, but we're not going to let them."

"I just hate waiting for something bad to happen."

"Then don't wait. Live."

He kissed her softly at first then harder as she moaned into him. She tasted of warmth and him, her tongue dancing with his, her breath coming in ragged pants.

Brayden pulled back, his breath equally as hard. "I love you, Ally. I know we're just starting out together, but I've always loved you. I don't want you to leave my home, not now, not ever. No, don't say anything. Just let me love you, touch you, please you. We can talk later, but right now, I need to feel you around me in every way possible."

He knew he wasn't being fair by not letting her say what might be on her mind, but he didn't care. He needed her more than anything, and, fuck, she looked sexy with her lips all swollen from his kisses, her eyes wide and dark for him.

Allison only nodded, and he took that as the yes he needed before crushing his mouth to hers, kissing her for all they were worth and more. He walked them back to the kitchen bar and lifted her up with a squeal of protest escaping from her lips.

He stripped her quickly, tearing at her clothes as she lifted his shirt over his head. He toed off his shoes then shucked his pants right along with his boxer briefs. He knew they were in his kitchen, bare-assed naked, but he didn't care. He wanted to quench his hunger, and this seemed like the perfect place to do it.

"Brayden, stop, I want to taste you. You promised."

He smiled and kissed her, running his hands down her sides, cupping her breasts, her nipples hardening against his palms.

"If that's what you want."

She snorted and wiggled off the counter, sinking to her knees. "Yeah, like you're going to turn down a blow job."

"I think I like it when you talk dirty."

She raised a brow. "Really?" She gripped his cock and squeezed. He closed his eyes on a moan. "So you like when I say I want to swallow your cock?"

"Fuck yeah."

"You know I've only talked dirty to you."

He opened his eyes and looked down. "Damn straight. And I'm going to be the *only* man you ever talk dirty to."

She didn't say anything but licked up his cock, forcing him to tangle his fingers in her long, auburn hair for control.

He held her loosely as she teased the head then swallowed him. She couldn't fit all of him into her mouth, but what she couldn't fit she rubbed with her hand. Fuck, she was damn good at this. He tightened the grip on her hair, and she gasped around his cock. He watched as her free hand drifted down to rub her clit.

"Jesus, that's hot. Rub yourself, baby while I fuck this pretty mouth." He held her still in his grip, and he thrust his dick between her swollen lips. He kept up a rapid pace before his balls tightened and his cock throbbed, ready to explode.

"I'm going to come down that throat, and you're going to swallow it all. Okay?"

She nodded around him, her hand working vigorously on her pussy. He knew she was as close as he was to coming he came, his cum filling her mouth and running down her throat. He watched as her pupils dilated, and a blush rose on her cheeks and her breasts as she came.

Brayden pulled out of her mouth, his seed dripping down her chin. Her little pink tongue darted out to catch the last drops.

"That was the hottest thing I've ever seen."

She smiled as he pulled her up to sit on the counter again.

"How are you still hard?" she finally said, her chest heaving with arousal.

He rolled her nipples in his hands, pleased when she gasped as he tweaked them harder than usual.

"Because you're fucking hot. And mine. I'm going to fuck you hard here then take you to the bedroom and eat you until you scream my name. How does that sound?"

"Like I can't wait."

The head of his dick probed her entrance, and he cursed. "I need to get a condom."

She reached down and gripped him. "We're both clean, and it will be hard for me to conceive." A shadow passed over her eyes, and he tried to kiss it away.

"And if we make a baby?" he asked, his body still as he waited for her response. Her next words could cement his future.

"Then we do."

"I'll take care of you. Of all of you. No matter what."

"I trust you."

He entered her slowly, not as hard as he'd promised. The idea of a future, her round with his child, her smiling as he loved her filled him, causing him to want to make this slow and special. There would be time for hard later.

They made love at a pace that worked for them, their gazes never wavering as they both came again, their bodies sweaty, sated.

Brayden loved this woman with everything he had, and he knew now that there was a future for them. She trusted him, something that he knew was hard for her.

This was his family, and he'd do anything to protect it.

Chapter 10

Allison wiped down the counter one last time and surveyed the empty diner. Her body ached from the night before when Brayden had loved her in so many delicious ways. She still couldn't believe she'd gone down on him right in the kitchen. She had spent the morning scrubbing that place clean, though she knew she'd be blushing during meals for a long time.

The thought of him put her in a frenzy, and she lost all control and inhibitions with him. She trusted him with her body, her heart, and her family—something she didn't think would ever be possible. There was no doubt in her mind that Brayden was the right man for her, and now she was just starting to feel more confident in thinking that they had a future.

She'd been scared when she saw him and Aiden walk out together to talk. Her oldest son had made it clear just with his expressions that he hadn't been completely on board with her new relationship. Not that she blamed him, considering all he'd seen as a child with Greg.

She cursed her weakness for staying with Greg, even if it had been magic compelling her to do so, making her stay with him and making her forget she wanted to leave.

When Aiden and Brayden had come back into the house, she'd seen the pact between them as a visible physical bond. At least that trial had been overcome, and they seemed to be working on it. Her kids would be back at the house today when she got home, and she'd be able to see fully how they reacted to Brayden being in their lives. At least she'd look at Aiden. Lacy and Cam were settled with him no matter what—something that thrilled and scared her at the same time. Aiden was the reluctant one, or at least had been. If he could get through it and want Brayden in their lives, then maybe this could work. They'd already gotten a taste of it over the past days, and she wanted to see if they would be okay with them moving in together.

Allison smiled. Oh, yes, she wanted this to happen. She trusted Brayden. Her new trust was a far cry from her fear before all of this started. She'd endured more than her fair share of heartache and pain, and now she was ready to give in and love...be loved.

She knew he wanted to marry her—something she'd never in her life thought she'd do again. And when he asked, she'd say yes.

A smile broke out over her face, and she let a giggle escape.

Everything had moved so fast, yet in the scheme of things, she'd waited forever for him, as he had for her.

God, she knew she looked like a freaking Barbie because she couldn't quit smiling, but she didn't care. All she wanted to do was go home and be with her family—Brayden included. But, not yet, since she had to work. Though Brayden had told her she was welcome to quit her job if she wanted to, she'd refused. She didn't want to be a kept woman.

She snorted.

Wow, now she sounded like an eighties romance heroine.

She wanted to pay her way, even if the contribution wasn't much.

She walked to the last of her tables and cleaned up their trash and the meager dollar tip. At least it was something. Though sometimes she hated the lulls at the diner because it meant no money, today she needed it because she wanted to just think.

Just breathe.

The cook had run to the store for something—probably cigarettes—so she was alone at the diner. Her kids were safe, with Cooper eyes on them at all times, and that's what mattered.

Allison started loading the dishwasher, put the food away, got the trash ready to take out and was just about to start a fresh pot of coffee for the next rush when the skin on her arms tingled, and she froze.

Two people stood in the doorway, a man and a woman who looked to be in their late fifties....and they looked pissed.

"Can I help you?" Allison asked, her voice surprisingly steady.

The man spoke first, his voice low, deep, and creepy as hell. "I'm Gerald Malone, you bitch."

Allison's eyes widened, but she wasn't surprised at the admission. She'd known who they were from the moment she'd seen Gerald. With his narrow nose and pointy chin, he looked too much like Greg and David to be anyone else.

"Gerald, do be quiet," the woman scolded lightly. "I'm Marline Malone. You killed both of our sons. You let our Greg die in a car accident and killed David with your own hand. Do you really think you can prance around in this fucking town filled with magic that has nothing to do with you?"

Allison raised her chin and cursed herself for leaving her cell phone in the break room. "I don't think what I do has anything to do with you."

They stepped farther into the diner as they laughed. Gerald slid the lock into place and turned the sign to closed.

"Oh, dear, it has *everything* to do with us," Marline explained. "We didn't want Greg to marry you, and yet he went against our wishes. Though I hear he tried to beat that dirtiness out of you, so that at least makes up for it."

Bile rose in Allison's throat, but she didn't move. She couldn't show any weakness, though really, she had no idea what she was going to do. She could only pray she could stall them long enough before they implemented their plan—whatever that might be. If enough time passed, hopefully the lunch rush would begin and her cook, Jason, would come back.

If only.

Marline walked closer, her beady black eyes looking more mythical than human. "You're nothing. You're just a human, and you will *not* raise those children. They're *mine*."

"No, they're mine. You may be a blood relation, but you cut off all ties before. They are *my* babies. You can't have them—the law won't let you."

"You think the law will stop us?" Gerald asked as he pulled out a long knife from his back pocket.

Oh, God.

"I see we have your attention," Marline said. "Once you're dead, we'll have your babies as their grandparents. There isn't anything you can do about it."

She swallowed hard, looking for a way out of this. "They'll know it was you." Brayden would know, and he'd take care of her babies.

"We'll make it look like a botched robbery." Gerald shrugged then licked his lips. "Though that doesn't mean we won't stop and play with you a bit. That's my favorite part after a kill. We even got past those little cops that sheriff of Holiday put on us. Like they could stop us."

Marline rolled her eyes. "That man and his playthings. Okay, fine, Gerald. You can cut her up some, but not too deep until the final kill. Make her suffer."

Gerald nodded then walked toward her.

Allison bolted toward the kitchen and the back door, but suddenly she froze. Her arms snapped against her sides, her throat closing as she fought for breath. Her back straightened, her legs coming together forcefully. It was as if someone had held her down, forcing her to not move.

Magic.

He pulled her body with an invisible rope to the kitchen and she held back a whimper.

"We're fucking gnomes," Marline spat. "We can make you do what we want. I can watch my husband rape you, and you'll want it. Do you really think we'll just let you run away?"

Allison's body forcibly turned toward her captors, and tears slid down her cheeks.

"We could force you to give us your kids, but then we'd have to make sure we kept the magic going continually, and that's a pain in the ass. I'd rather just have my husband kill you. After he has his fun."

Revulsion slid through her as Gerald slowly cut into her arm. Sharp pain sliced through her, even though she couldn't move. She was frozen, but she wasn't numb. Though she couldn't move no matter how much she tried, she felt every slice and every drop of blood flowing. Fear clawed at her, her body trying to shake out of nerves, but couldn't because they held her down. She smelled the stale stench of his breath as he leaned close, enjoying his work.

Allison tried to move, but it was no use.

They'd kill her and take her babies.

She couldn't give up...but what could she do?

She closed her eyes as he pressed the blade harder. Brayden's face filled her vision.

Brayden.

****

The coin around Brayden's neck heated, scalding his skin, and he cursed as he slid out from under the car he'd been working on. He pulled the leather cord from his neck and looked down at the coin.

It burned red hot, something it'd never done before.

What the hell?

The ridges on the edge seem to rise even higher, as if trying to tell him something. He'd always known the heat meant something was coming, but this was different. He could feel the indentions of the symbols and words on the coin rise up and heat. This was something important. But what.

The coin had only heated when luck was needed, when he was stressed or when he was needed, not when he was just hanging around working. Did that mean he should be concentrating on something else? Something he might need help in controlling?

Something was wrong... he felt as though someone might be in trouble. He couldn't explain it, but he had a bad feeling. He'd always had a feeling when something was about to be good for him, but this was new. Wrong. He knew the kids were safe since one of his brothers would have called if that weren't the case.

That left only Allison.

Fuck.

He wiped as much of the grease off his hands as possible and ran to his truck, past his employees with their astonished expressions, knowing they had to think he was crazy as hell. Maybe he was. But his coin was still hot, though not as red-hot as before, so he must be on the right track.

Maybe.

After all, he was following his gut and a coin a leprechaun had given him as a kid. What could go wrong?

He drove like a bat out of hell the seven minutes it took to get to the diner and cursed as he noticed the closed sign. It was the middle of the day, and he knew the lunch rush would happen at any moment. Allison wouldn't have changed the sign herself.

Brayden jumped out of the truck, leaving it running and the door open and sprinted to the door. Brayden pulled, only to find it locked, and peered through the glass. He didn't see anything, but the over-turned stool made his blood freeze.

He couldn't see Allison, but he knew she was in there. How, he didn't know. Stealing himself, he took a step back, kicked as hard as he could, sending glass across the room and into his skin, then ran through the glass shards. He barely felt the pain as he ran to the kitchen, not knowing what he'd find.

What he found was unimaginable.

She lay on the kitchen floor, a pool of blood around her, her body pale, her eyes wide. Shallow cuts covered her arms and side from what he could see through her uniform. She was on her back, her hair in wild disarray around her.

"Brayden," she mouthed.

He ran to her, kneeling in her blood and cursing the wounds that marred her body.

"Ally."

Jesus. What had this person done to her? Oh, he thought he knew who it could be, but he didn't know for sure. She had to be in a tremendous amount of pain, but he didn't know what to do. Did he move her? Did he cover her? He kissed her brow, lightly running his hand though her hair, afraid to touch anything else. Fuck, why couldn't it have been him? He'd have done anything to be the one in pain.

"You're an idiot, you know," a woman's voice said from behind him. "You really should check your surroundings before you barge into a room with a cut-up bitch on the floor."

Brayden's coin heated, and he ducked instinctively as a knife swept over him.

"Fuck," the man yelled when he missed.

Brayden gripped his coin and rolled, pulling a moaning Allison with him. Every time the man swiped, he missed, and Brayden thanked his coin for that.

"Why are you here?" Brayden asked, barely able to think beyond Allison and the rage filling him.

"We want the children. Just give them to us, and we won't hurt you," the woman said as she stared at him, but Brayden could see the fear in her eyes.

Bray gripped the coin around his neck. "You recognize this, don't you?"

The man backed away, but snorted. "A lucky trinket. It means nothing since you aren't one of the magic folk yourself."

"But, I still have the magic running in my veins. I'm still stronger than those you prey on, and I won't let you hurt my family."

"Your family?" the woman asked. "They're *my* blood. Their mother's a whore for fucking you with no thought."

"Watch your mouth," Brayden said as he felt Allison move beside him. Her movement gave him hope.

"You will not have those kids!" the woman screamed and came at him, her hands raised, magic like a stream of inky black mixed with the most plum of violets pouring out of her.

Intuitively, Brayden held up his arms, protecting Allison and himself. The coin around his neck warmed, and a blast of gold light spread out, encircling them in a bubble of protection. The woman screamed again, this time in terror and pain, as her power ricocheted back and hit her, her body catching on fire in a burst of bright, glittering gold.

"Brayden?" Allison asked, her voice weak. "What's happening?"

"I don't know, baby."

The woman continued screaming, frantically trying to quell the flames, but it was no use. The flames engulfed her, leaving only a trail of gold dust in their wake. The man cried out in pain and scooped up her dust, his body catching on fire just like his wife's had.

Brayden twisted, covering Allison with his body, not sure if the fire would spread and take them, too.

But, soon the sounds of a mass stampede echoed in the kitchen as his brothers entered, their faces pale and eyes wide.

"What the fuck?" Tyler asked as he rushed in, his gun in his hand.

Brayden lifted away from Allison. "Jesus, baby, we need to get you to the doctor."

"I'm fine."

"No, no, you're not." He leaned down and kissed her softly, aware she had to hurt all over.

"Don't touch that, Justin," Tyler said as the leaned over the gold dust that had once been gnomes. "The Malones used fucking magic to get around the cops I had on their house. Fuck, I'm sorry, man."

As they watched, the dust faded away to nothing, leaving only a very confused group of people and a hurt Allison in its wake.

"What the hell just happened?" Matt asked.

"I don't know," Brayden said, "but right now we need to get Ally to the hospital." Even as he said it, his coin heated, and he knew what to do.

He took it off his neck and carefully lifted her head and put the cord around her neck. Her eyes widened as a gold dusting covered her body like a slow wave cascading along her. The skin around her cuts stitched themselves together then faded away. The gold dust seeped into her skin and she lay there as his Allison—fresh and whole.

"What did you do?" she asked. "That was yours!"

"Now it's yours."

"But...I don't understand anything that just happened."

"I don't either, but we'll talk about it later. I just need to get you home."

Home. Their home.

"But, Bray, this was yours." She fingered the coin at her neck, but he watched only her even as he heard his brothers surveying the diner dealing with the practical things like the broken door and curious people.

"You're my luck, Ally-mine."

He leaned down and kissed her, knowing his luck had nothing to do with the coin but everything to do with the woman in his arms.

Chapter 11

"For honor and country!" Cameron yelled as he jumped on Brayden's back, bringing him to the floor.

Brayden rolled, making sure he landed on the bottom so he didn't hurt Cameron. "You'll never get me!" he yelled back then grunted as Lacy dove into his side.

"I'll protect you, Daddy," she squealed, and Brayden choked, letting Cameron pummel his fists into his side.

Daddy.

That was the second time she'd called him that, and each time a little part of him fell that much more in love with her. Cam and Aiden hadn't called him dad yet, but he was okay with that. It'd been only two days since the Malones had come to town and threatened his family. Everyone was still shaken about what they'd seen and the power the coin held. But, Allison still wore it around her neck to her chagrin and his insistence.

They were making themselves a family...though he hadn't even proposed to Ally yet. Something he'd have to fix soon.

He looked over Cam's and Lacy's heads at Allison. She smiled at him, tears in her eyes and her arm around Aiden's shoulder.

Aid gave him a thumbs-up then ran to help Justin man the grill. Brayden rolled around with the other two for a few more minutes before getting to his knees, his hands up.

"Okay, you win."

"Yes!" Cam pumped his fist then high-fived Lacy.

Lacy wrapped her arms around Brayden's neck and kissed his cheek before whispering in his ear, "I was working on both sides, but I love you more."

Touched beyond all measure, he tugged Lacy close to him and inhaled that sweet, little-girl scent that made him want to protect her from all the bad things in life...as well as any boys that might dare come near her in the future.

Apparently that's what being a father felt like.

Oh, he liked it.

A lot.

Aiden came running back in, and Allison pulled him close. Brayden stayed on his knees, one arm wrapped around Cam's shoulders, the other holding Lacy to him. He knew it was past time... no, the perfect time to do this.

"Allison?"

The use of her full name had her staring at him as though he were crazy. "Yes?"

"I know I should probably wait until we're alone...but this is about more than just the two of us. So I'm asking all of you.

Her eyes filled with tears as he noticed the rest of his family coming around them, smiles on their faces.

"Allison, Aiden, Cameron, and Lacy, will you marry me and make me the happiest—and luckiest—man I could be? Please say yes."

"Yes!" Lacy answered and kissed his cheek again.

He laughed, and his family joined him. Cameron hugged his other side, and Aiden tugged his mother toward Brayden.

"Ally?" he asked, a little bit of fear creeping in because she wasn't saying anything.

"Oh, yes, Brayden. Yes, yes, yes." She fell to her knees, Aiden coming with her, and she hugged him. The five of them wrapped their arms around each other, tears running down all their faces. Eventually, the rest of the Coopers joined them on the floor, and they laughed and congratulated them.

"It's about freaking time," Justin teased.

He looked up as Allison brushed the coin around her neck, a smile on her face. "I love you," she whispered. "This coin? It's ours. Not yours. Not mine. Ours."

"I'm the luckiest guy on earth, and I'd take all the time in the world to keep my luck and our life."

Allison kissed him hard, and he knew all was right. After all, since he didn't have the coin around his neck, he'd just have to make his own luck from now on. Or maybe he could just borrow a little bit from his new wife.

ABOUT THE AUTHOR

Carrie Ann Ryan is a bestselling paranormal and contemporary romance author. After spending too much time behind a lab bench, she decided to dive into the romance world and find her werewolf mate - even if it's just in her books. Happy endings are always near - even if you have to get over the challenges of falling in love first.

Carrie Ann's Redwood Pack series is a bestselling series that has made the shifter world even more real to her and has allowed the Dante's Circle and Holiday, Montana series to be born. She's also an avid reader and lover of romance and fiction novels. She loves meeting new authors and new worlds. Any recommendations you have are appreciated. Carrie Ann lives in New England with her husband and two kittens.

www.carrieannryan.com

Printed in Great Britain
by Amazon.co.uk, Ltd.,
Marston Gate.